"Special Agent Logan Pierce. I need you to come with me."

Zara's jaw dropped. *"What?"*

"No time to explain. The first priority is to get you somewhere safe." The fingers of his hand wrapped around her upper arm like a steel band. He swiftly propelled her along with him to a distant exit.

"Safe! What the—"

She was accompanying a strange man—a very large and intimidating strange man—to God knew where, for God knew what purpose.

Zara jerked hard against his unyielding grip, to no avail. "Hold on," she cried. "Mr. Pierce! I mean, Agent Pierce, please!" She tried to sound assertive. "I need to see your ID again."

"No time."

Her voice wobbled as they sprinted across the parking lot. "Why do you have to get me somewhere safe. Safe from what? From who?"

He stopped, but he did not release her. His features were strong, intriguing. His big body radiated heat and male vitality. "You should be more careful who you do business with."

Dear Reader,

When Harlequin asked us to write two books featuring twin heroines, they didn't have to ask twice! As identical twins ourselves, we knew we'd have a blast with this unique project.

Along with the creative challenge came a geographical one: We live four hundred miles apart! However, between occasional road trips and daily phone calls (our twin telepathy was on the fritz), we brainstormed a dynamite suspense story that begins in *Twice the Spice,* Pat's Harlequin Temptation (April '97), and ends here in Pam's *Twice Burned.*

While each book stands on its own, we urge you to read both for the most enjoyment. We've woven tender romance and sizzling passion into a story rife with mistaken identity, heart-thumping danger, stunning plot twists and more than one dark secret.

Our twin heroines, Emma and Zara, are close to our hearts. Despite different personalities and a strained relationship, their special bond gives them the strength and courage to overcome all odds. And as for Gage and Logan...we think you'll fall in love with them both, just as we did!

We'd love to hear from you. Write to us at P.O. Box 1321, North Baldwin, NY 11510-0721 (send an SASE for a reply).

Happy reading!

Sincerely,

Pamela Burford and Patricia Ryan

Twice Burned
Pamela Burford

Harlequin Books

TORONTO • NEW YORK • LONDON
AMSTERDAM • PARIS • SYDNEY • HAMBURG
STOCKHOLM • ATHENS • TOKYO • MILAN
MADRID • WARSAW • BUDAPEST • AUCKLAND

To the "good twin," Patricia Ryan,
for never letting me forget that
life is not a dress rehearsal

ISBN 0-373-22420-6

TWICE BURNED

Copyright © 1997 by Pamela Loeser

This edition published by arrangement with Harlequin Books S.A.

® and TM are trademarks of the publisher. Trademarks indicated with ® are registered in the United States Patent and Trademark Office, the Canadian Trade Marks Office and in other countries.

Printed in U.S.A.

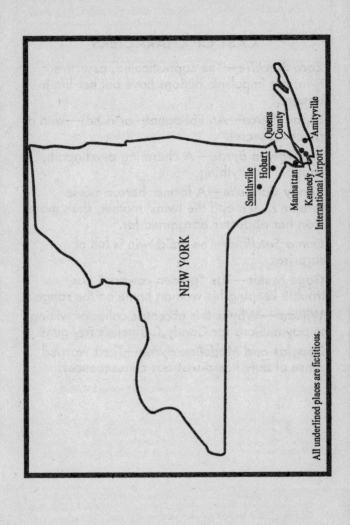

Smithville
Hobart

NEW YORK

Queens
County

Amityville

Manhattan
Kennedy
International Airport

All underlined places are fictitious.

CAST OF CHARACTERS

Zara Sutcliffe—The sophisticated, assertive twin; her impulsive actions have put her life in danger.

Logan Pierce—An FBI agent—or is he?—with a shocking secret.

MacGowan Byrne—A charming psychopath, capable of anything.

Candy Carmelle—A former horror-movie scream queen and the twins' mother, she's more than her abductor bargained for.

Emma Sutcliffe—The timid twin is full of surprises.

Gage Foster—The "golden cowboy" has trouble keeping his woman home on the range.

William—Why is this eccentric collector willing to pay millions for Candy Carmelle's ray gun?

Douglas and Madeline Byrne—Their warped sense of duty has disastrous consequences.

Chapter One

Wolf's eyes, Zara thought, watching the man weave through the crowd at Kennedy Airport's International Arrivals Building, that feral golden brown gaze riveted to her.

It struck her then, where she'd seen those eyes. In that painting of a timber wolf that used to hang in her father's den.

A little shiver scuttled up her spine. Exhaustion, she told herself. The flight from Sydney to New York had been interminable, and she'd yet to refine the art of sleeping on planes. On top of that, the geek in customs had given her short, tight-fitting fuchsia suit a lingering once-over and made her wait another half hour while he took his time pawing through her luggage and ogling her cleavage.

Now she wanted nothing more than to cab it back to her penthouse apartment on East Eighty-sixth and soak the kinks away in an aroma-therapeutic whirlpool bath. Maybe she'd call her masseuse.

She grimaced, remembering her masseuse was a thing of the past, thanks to Tony. Her ex-husband's greed and vindictiveness had left her emotionally and financially drained. She'd lost even the privacy she so desperately craved, since she now lacked the means to install her mother in a place of her own.

With any luck, Mom would be out bowling or something and Zara would have a few rare minutes of solitary peace.

With even more luck, her twin sister, Emma, wouldn't have bollixed up the transaction Zara had arranged. The transaction that would give her back her privacy.

Wolf Eyes was nearly upon her now, striding with single-minded resolve. He was hard to ignore, towering over everyone else by at least half a head, his dark hair pulled back in a ponytail, those eerie, unsmiling eyes locked on her like heat-seeking missiles.

She sighed. What now?

Whatever business he had with her, it could wait till Monday, and office hours. She refused to deal with it now, when she was mentally fried and both her Movado watch and her internal clock were set at Sydney time. She rationalized that since she'd already made it to Saturday morning, she could ignore this pushy fellow who was still getting through Friday afternoon.

He was probably some hack author who took exception to receiving a form rejection letter from the Zara Sutcliffe Literary Agency.

She tried to veer away from him, but her progress was hampered by the gigantic wheeled Hartmann suitcase she was hauling, with assorted smaller matching bags dangling from it by straps.

Suddenly he was there, planted directly in her path like some damn sequoia, blocking her escape route.

She skidded to a graceless stop in her stiletto heels, nearly landing on her fanny when the heavy suitcase rolled into her, driven by forward momentum.

Rather than reaching out to steady her, as any gentleman would have done, Wolf Eyes flashed an open badge wallet in her face.

"Special Agent Logan Pierce. FBI. I need you to come with me, Miss Sutcliffe."

Zara's jaw dropped and she gaped at him like a beached mackerel. *"What?"*

He reached around her and seized the handle of her suitcase. "No time to explain. The first priority is to get you somewhere safe."

"Safe! What the—"

The fingers of his free hand wrapped around her upper arm like a steel band. He swiftly propelled her along with him toward the distant exit.

They were halfway there when the shock wore off and her mind lurched into high gear. She was accompanying a strange man—a very large and intimidating strange man—to God knew where, for God knew what purpose. He didn't even look like an FBI agent. Didn't G-men wear suits and ties? This guy was in jeans and a black windbreaker over a maroon T-shirt.

Zara jerked hard against his unyielding grip, to no avail. He didn't even slow his pace. He towed her ponderous luggage with such apparent ease, it might have been a toddler's pull toy.

"Hold on!" she cried. "Wait up a minute."

No response. Those stony wolf's eyes never stopped scanning the noisy crowd, for what hidden perils, she could only imagine.

"Mr. Pierce! I mean, Agent Pierce, please!" She

twisted her arm where his long fingers crushed the silk. "You're hurting me."

"You're hurting yourself. Take it easy."

"*Take it easy?* Listen, mister, if you don't let go of me this instant and tell me what this is about, I swear I'll scream my head off."

He stopped, but he didn't release her. He stared down at her, his expression revealing impatience and more than a little distaste. His features were strong, not classically handsome but interesting.

Okay, intriguing. She couldn't help it. Behind those cool amber eyes she detected more stories than one man had a right to.

She almost laughed at the fanciful notion. Her imagination would be the death of her yet. If she could write worth a damn, she'd be a novelist herself instead of a literary agent.

She tried to sound assertive. "I need to see your ID again."

"No time." He was off once more, Zara's spiked heels clicking on the tiled floor as he hauled her along, just another piece of baggage.

Outside the terminal, the air was balmy, the sky clear azure—a flawless May afternoon. Zara squinted against the dazzling sun, wishing she could get to her shades. Somehow she doubted Pierce would be willing to stop and let her fish them out of her carry-on.

They crossed busy airport roads, darting through traffic. All the while he continued to scrutinize their surroundings.

Suddenly it occurred to her that his loose windbreaker almost certainly concealed a holster. She swallowed back a knot of apprehension. Her voice wobbled as they sprinted across the parking lot. "You said you had to get me somewhere safe. Safe from what? From who?"

"MacGowan Byrne."

She lost her precarious footing as that sank in, and would have ended up sprawled on the pavement if not for Pierce's death grip on her arm.

"Mac Byrne?" she squeaked. "The art dealer?" The man she'd made Emma promise to meet to complete the lucrative sale she'd arranged? The man who was going to solve all her financial problems?

"That's the one." He retrieved a key chain and thumbed a keyless entry button. A car chirped nearby. A small, sleek BMW. Black with tinted windows and wide tires. He quickly stowed her luggage in the trunk, then opened the passenger door and shoved her inside. She barely had time to pull in her feet before he slammed the door.

He circled the car and slid behind the wheel, his movements swift and economical, as graceful as the timber wolf she'd likened him to.

And no doubt as dangerous.

He seemed to completely fill the compact sports car, his big body radiating heat and male vitality. Turning the key, he said, "You should be more careful who you do business with. Mac Byrne tried to kill your sister when she went to meet with him."

"Emma?" she whispered.

Zara was drowning. Air. She needed air. She dug her nails into the leather armrest, her chest heaving with the effort to make her world stop reeling.

"Is she...is she okay?"

Pierce didn't spare her a glance. "She's no longer

in danger. But he's got your mother. Candy Carmelle. Kidnapped her from your apartment over a week ago."

A sob broke through the fingers she clamped over her mouth.

Dear God, what have I done?

A solid metallic snick made her jump. The sound of power door locks engaging. She glanced at the spot where her own lock button should have been, only to spy an empty hole. Her gaze flew to her companion's impassive profile as he palmed the steering wheel and backed out of the parking space.

"A little insurance."

CANDY CARMELLE WAS a dead woman. She could see it in her captor's cold, golden brown eyes. Wolf's eyes.

As she looked back on her sixty-one years, her only regret was having slept with Billy Sharke back in 1966 for the ray gun—the first step in a love affair that changed the course of her life. If it weren't for that damn ray gun, she'd be home right now, watching "Oprah" and working Lady Clairol into her roots.

Billy had directed her in *Dr. Blood, Blood Wedding, The Slithering, The Brain from Asteroid X, The Atomic Bride* and *Return of the Atomic Bride.* He'd adored Candy. No one could scream like her. She was the queen bee of B-movie scream queens. A regular diva.

Candy stared sullenly at the movie prop that had vanquished the Atomic Bride and her undead minions in *Return,* now tucked into a corner of the dingy basement room that had been her prison for more than a week. The ray gun was polished chrome, the size and approximate shape of a rifle. A 1950s version of a futuristic weapon, it sported more knobs, levers, gadgets and gizmos than the space shuttle.

She'd thought she was the only one with a sentimental attachment to the silly thing. Seems some weird recluse with more money than God just couldn't live without it. And Mac Byrne was more than willing to accommodate him.

She sneaked a peek at Mac, who'd just come in from one of his mysterious excursions. He sat slumped at the opposite end of the rump-sprung sofa that doubled as her bed, staring into middle distance and muttering to himself. She thought she heard ripe cussing directed at "that damn cowboy." Again.

No doubt about it, her captor was a few pecans short of a pie and getting loonier by the hour.

Maybe that "damn cowboy" was the one who'd worked Mac over shortly after he kidnapped Candy from her daughter Zara's apartment. Mac had hog-tied her and left her in this musty cellar for what seemed like hours. She had to admit the terror and discomfort were almost worth it when he returned looking like rewarmed dog do—a split lip, a nasty shiner and a couple of cracked ribs.

Couldn't happen to a nicer psychopath.

If nothing else, the shellacking her captor had endured was evidence that all was not going according to his demented plans. Which might mean that her daughter Emma, Zara's twin sister, was still safe. Perhaps this "cowboy," whoever he was, was looking after her. Whatever else, Candy couldn't help but feel warm and fuzzy about anyone Mac hated so virulently.

"Mac...?" Her tone couldn't get more syrupy if she were gargling with molasses.

He slid her a suspicious sidelong glance.

She scooted closer. "Your face healed up nicely, but I bet those ribs are still bothering you. Lemme have a look."

She reached for his shirt. He grabbed her wrist, not roughly but with enough force to aggravate the rope burns. She winced. Immediately his touch turned gentle as he sat up and examined the welts.

He murmured, "Your skin is so delicate. These'll get infected if I don't put something on them. I'll go out for some ointment."

"Your hands are very soothing." She smiled shyly and traced the muscular pad of his thumb. "But strong, too. I find that so...intriguing. A man of contradictions."

Contradictions, hell, the guy was downright schizoid—brutally cold one second, tender and solicitous the next.

Sweet Lord, how had this demented creep talked Zara into selling him the ray gun in the first place? Her daughter was supposed to be an astute businesswoman. Candy liked the way they'd put it in that *Wall Street Journal* article:

Zara Sutcliffe is the quintessential nineties wheeler-dealer, a glamorous literary superagent with more media presence than her famous and infamous clients.

Candy often wished Zara's twin sister, Emma, possessed a fraction of that glamour—or the street smarts that went along with it. But then, it was staid, sensible Emma who'd been forced to cope with the desperate situation her impulsive sister had caused.

She studied Mac as he tenderly inspected her wrists. His display of concern was ludicrous—they both knew he had no intention of releasing her alive.

The man might be a homicidal maniac, but he was a good-looking, prosperous homicidal maniac. Mid-thirties, tall and powerfully built, with rugged features and long dark hair past his shoulders—and that Rolex didn't come from Kmart. On the surface, precisely the sort of affluent, studly hunk she'd always wanted Emma and Zara to hook up with.

He said, "I didn't want to do this to you, Candy. They left me no choice." Those wolflike eyes looked more like a puppy's now, anxious for her approval.

He'd abducted her to force Emma to hand over the ray gun. Now that he had it, he was supposed to release her. But Candy was under no illusions. She'd seen enough movies to know what happened to hostages who could identify their kidnappers.

They were never heard from again.

Her only hope was to stall for time. And the best way to accomplish that was to play on Mac's weakness: his adolescent fixation on Candy Carmelle, scream queen *extraordinaire*.

When he'd kidnapped her he was no doubt anticipating your basic sixtyish grandma type. What he'd ended up with was the same fit, alluring B-movie actress he'd obviously spent his youth drooling over, glued to the tube and *Reptile Bride* day after day on the "Million Dollar Movie."

She and Jane Fonda were about the same age, and the similarities didn't stop there. They were both shining examples of sexy mature womanhood. Candy even dreamed of starring in her own exercise videos, though that was all it amounted to, a dream. Her initial inquiries had left her dispirited.

Still, that goal had been something to fantasize about when she'd assumed she had a few more decades in which to grow old disgracefully. With every hour that passed, that future appeared more elusive. Well, she sure as hell wasn't going to give in without a fight. Her weapon of choice? The one she'd spent a lifetime honing.

She took a deep, shuddering breath and was pleased to note the direction of Mac's gaze. The top two buttons of her blouse had popped off during the struggle in Zara's apartment, revealing a deep vee of crimson lace and what Billy Sharke used to call ten pounds of cantaloupes in a five-pound sack.

She sank her pearly capped incisors into her collagen-enhanced lower lip, her full, shivering sigh a double-barreled testament to the wonders of modern medical science. She quickly averted her tear-glazed, nipped-and-tucked eyes, just as she'd done back in 1963 when the title creature in *The Undead Tongue* got a little too close for comfort.

"Aw, Candy…"

"I—" That little catch in her voice for effect. "I'm just so—so—frightened, Mac."

He released his breath in a rush and sagged into the sofa. Avoiding her eyes.

She was doomed.

Why hadn't she married Billy? She could've had him, he'd wanted to make it legal, but no, she had to go and *elevate* herself. That's where John Sutcliffe, investment banker, came in. Rambling estate in Connecticut. Piles of moldy Old Money. Hordes of snooty richer-than-thou friends.

And a mean streak that had no bounds.

She hadn't lasted two years. Leaving him was the biggest mistake of her life. By the time she realized John would never let her have the girls, it was too late. He wouldn't take her back. And she was no match for the high-powered lawyers all that Old Money could buy.

So she lost her twin daughters, Zara and Emma, her beautiful dark-haired babies. Didn't see them again till they were grown and came looking for her, after John's death.

Mac jumped up and paced to the far wall. "He was there, you know. He's there every time I turn around nowadays. I can feel him breathing down my neck, just waiting for me to slip up." He kicked a metal utility pail and sent it flying across the room.

Candy said, "Who? The cowboy?"

His gaze snapped to her and she bit her lip. Gone were the puppy-dog eyes. Here was the wolf, dangerous and unpredictable.

"No," he said slowly. "Not the cowboy." He stalked to the Peg-Board and grabbed the loop of rope hanging there.

A whimper of protest escaped her. He didn't always tie her when he left the house; it depended on his mood and the depth of his paranoia at the moment.

He had to know she was helpless either way. The one window was securely covered with thick plywood nailed to the fifties-style knotty pine paneling. The door at the top of the wooden stairs was bolted from the outside, and there was nothing in either her little prison or the adjacent bathroom that could be used as a weapon or to summon help.

He stood there for an indecisive moment, scowling at her abused wrists. Then he flung the rope to the tile floor. She let out a silent sigh of relief, careful to avoid eye contact. She'd already learned not to mess with him when he was like this. He could turn on her in a heartbeat.

Even when he did tie her, he never bothered gagging her, and she no longer wasted her breath hollering for help. Her talents as a scream queen were useless here in this isolated old house in a semirural area north of New York City. No neighbors within earshot.

Mac grabbed the ray gun and took the steps three at a time. Candy flinched when she heard the bolt slide home.

THE COCKROACH SKIRTED the edge of the bare mattress lying on the filthy concrete floor. It paused a moment, then crawled up onto the frayed ticking.

Zara shuddered. Pierce couldn't really expect her to *sleep* on that revolting thing, with its mildewy odor and suspicious-looking stains?

The cool, coarse floor tugged at her stockinged feet as she crossed to the long wall of grime-encrusted windows. It was nearly dark. The sky—what she could see of it above the windowless brick building across the street—was a deep purplish gray. One window was tipped open and she stuck her head out to feel the cool breeze on her face, to draw in a lungful of the foul New York City air she'd missed so much while she was in Australia.

She was five stories up in a deserted movers' warehouse in an industrial area of Manhattan. Somewhere in the Thirties near Tenth Avenue—she hadn't paid strict attention when they arrived three hours ago, preoccupied as she'd been with trying to pry information out of a taciturn Agent Pierce.

If he really was an FBI agent.

He'd escorted her up here, locked her in—for her protection, he'd said—and left immediately. He hadn't even had the decency to bring her luggage up from the car. For three hours she'd had only her overactive imagination for company.

And her guilt.

If Pierce was to be believed, Zara's mother had been kidnapped. By Mac Byrne, the same maniac who'd tried to kill her twin sister, Emma.

This whole mess was her own fault. She closed her eyes and slumped against the window, the glass cool against her forehead. It was she who'd put the ball in motion by jumping at Mac's offer to buy Candy's ray gun. She should have known it was too good to be true.

Two million dollars.

The strident sound of the dead bolt kick-started her heart. Pierce materialized on the threshold, a shadowy figure filling the doorway.

"It's dark in here." His deep voice rumbled across the cavernous room and rolled over her, through her.

She swallowed hard. "I—I didn't know if it was safe to turn on lights."

He crossed the room in a few long strides, leaving a tantalizing aroma in his wake. A cluster of abandoned furniture occupied one corner, including the unsavory mattress. The floor lamp winked on—a retro-looking throwback to the sixties. She was glad he hadn't turned on the overhead fluorescent lights. He deposited a white paper sack on the chipped, boomerang-shaped Formica coffee table.

"If you're a vegetarian, you're outta luck," he said.

"I'm not." She didn't budge.

He unzipped his windbreaker and shrugged out of it. Even though she was prepared, the sight of his shoulder holster strapped over the maroon T-shirt startled her. The wide brown leather straps hugged his shoulders front and back in a kind of halter design. A black gun grip peeked out from the burnished leather under his arm.

He kept it on.

He dragged a straight chair closer to the table, sat and began emptying the bags. Without looking up, he said, "You gonna stand there all night?"

She locked her knees against a deep shiver. What was it about this man that made her feel so utterly exposed?

When they had yet to exchange fifty words!

He raised his head and those glowing golden eyes found her, skewered her. Challenged her.

She forced herself to put one foot in front of the other. The rough floor fought her progress, snagging her stockings. Each tentative step felt like a cold, clinging kiss on the soles of her feet, urging her to retreat.

He watched her steadily as she entered the circle of light thrown by the floor lamp. That assessing gaze missed nothing, from her short, dark, stylishly cut hair down to the tiny runs racing up her black silk stockings.

The inspection was thorough but not lewd. In the instant before he returned his attention to his dinner, she detected a hint of disdain. As if, indeed, he saw right through the glamorous, self-possessed facade she'd so painstakingly erected. Most men were downright intimidated by that facade—the look, the attitude, the trappings of fame and success. The whole beauty-and-brains thing.

Why couldn't Logan Pierce be one of those men?

She stared at the meal he'd laid out on the dusty table. Two large bundles wrapped in white deli paper. A couple of plastic salad containers. Plastic-wrapped carrot cake and two bottles of iced tea.

"The Sicilian's for you," he said.

"The what?"

"That's what the deli down the street calls it." He unwrapped one of the bundles and lifted the top of a hero roll to reveal the motley contents. "Genoa salami, pepperoni, mortadella, provolone," he recited. "Lettuce, tomato, onions, olive oil and vinegar. The whole shebang." Those cool eyes flicked over her. "I figured, since you're part Italian."

She blinked. A lucky guess, or was there a file at FBI headquarters labeled Sutcliffe, Zara?

Perhaps that file included the little-known tidbits about her mother that had never made it into the film fanzines. Such as her Italian heritage. In 1957 beautiful, determined Giovanna Sarro bought herself a one-way bus ticket from New York's Little Italy to Hollywood, where she soon learned to mix peroxide with celluloid and remade herself as Candy Carmelle.

Zara wanted to ask what else he knew, but instead said, "What are you having?"

Wordlessly he opened his hard roll and showed her a pile of ultrarare roast beef slathered with brown mustard. The roll was stained red from the meat.

She grimaced. "Still twitching, I see." She peered into the empty bag. "Paper plates? For the slaw and potato salad?"

Mouth full, he shrugged and indicated the plastic forks. As if he expected the two of them to just dig in to the same container.

How cozy.

She looked around for another chair and came up empty. "Listen, Pierce, I'm kinda curious."

"Most people call me Logan."

"Logan, then. You called this place a safe house. I always thought a safe house was supposed to be, like, a *house?*"

He studied her as he chewed and swallowed, then chased the wad of raw cow with a long pull of iced tea. "I always thought the operative word was *safe.* Sit down and eat."

She eyed the mattress with distaste, wishing Logan were gentleman enough to offer her the chair. She gingerly lowered herself onto the very edge of the thin mattress, clamping her knees and ankles together while trying to squirm into some semblance of a ladylike posture. Nevertheless, her short, snug skirt rode way up, displaying the tops of her stockings, black satin garter clasps and a healthy expanse of thigh. She yanked on the skirt, to no avail.

Logan, staring down from his perch next to her, had a spectacular view of the action. She was certain he could see not only her garter belt but her black thong panties, as well. Sitting there under that bright floor lamp, she felt like Sharon Stone being interrogated in *Basic Instinct.*

Except Sharon had been in control. She certainly hadn't been wriggling and swearing like this, wrenching at her recalcitrant clothing. And Michael Douglas had had the grace to be embarrassed. This bastard just sat there watching her, calmly devouring that damn bleeding thing he called a sandwich!

She squeezed her knees together and splayed her ankles, grunting and sweating as she tried to lever herself off the mattress. *"Help me up!"* She reached out a hand.

"Do I have to?"

So he did know how to smile. She'd assumed his face would fracture with the effort.

Before she could spit out a reply, he seized her wrist and easily hoisted her to her feet.

She gritted, "I don't suppose I could bother you for my luggage. If I'm going to be stuck here awhile, I'd like to change into something less...something more..."

"Practical?" He got up and strode to the door. "Leave me some coleslaw."

Logan returned in less than two minutes. He dumped her elegant matched bags near one of the concrete-reinforced columns studding the room, next to his enormous battered green duffel and a couple of sleeping bags. "There you go."

She hoisted one eyebrow and sneered, "Aren't you going to search my luggage?"

"Did that earlier."

"*What!*" She'd been kidding!

"Go change. The john's over there."

"I know where it is." She stalked toward her large Pullman bag and started pulling out clothes. "I found it while you were gone. For three hours!"

"Missed me, did you?"

She shot back, "Are you really an FBI agent?"

He never blinked. "If I'm not, it's a little too late for you to do anything about it now."

Chapter Two

When she emerged from the bathroom the lamplit corner was deserted. She peered into the shadows and finally located Logan at the windows. He held something to his ear—a tiny cellular phone. His voice was a deep murmur; she couldn't make out the words. As he conversed, he scanned the street below, making her wonder for the first time just how safe this safe house was.

He turned, and though she couldn't see his face, she knew he was staring at her.

She had to admit it felt like heaven to get out of those stockings and that constricting suit she'd worn all the way from Sydney. She'd changed into a loose calf-length skirt of sand-washed silk in shades of turquoise and ivory. The supple fabric flowed around her bare legs like a whisper. Over it she wore a long ivory tunic of raw silk. It was the most comfortable outfit she owned, and the most subdued. A far cry from the sexy power suit that was her usual uniform.

He said, "Hang on, Lou," and addressed Zara. "You go in Saturdays, right? To the office?"

"Sure. Almost every week." She crossed to her suitcase and stuffed her travel clothes in it.

"Sundays, too," he said, as if he knew her schedule, and just wanted confirmation.

"Sundays, too." Why did he need to know this?

He turned his back to her and spoke in low tones to Lou, whoever he was. The phone closed with a snap and he pushed the antenna in with his palm.

She said, "They're going to miss me at my office if I don't call—"

"It's already taken care of. As far as your employees are concerned, you had to return to Australia and will be out of touch for a while."

She stared at him, outraged at his presumption. "Define 'a while.'"

Instead, he changed the subject. "If you're so hard up for cash, why are you still holding on to that second apartment in L.A.?" He strode across the room and tossed the phone on the mattress. "Ever since your divorce, you spend all your time at the office anyway."

His casual observation clawed at wounds that were still raw after eighteen months. She closed her eyes for a few moments, willing the bitter memories back into the dark place in her soul reserved for her failures. It was getting pretty crowded in there.

She took a deep breath. "I need a place to stay on the coast. I'm out there all the time, negotiating book-movie deals for my clients." She joined him at the coffee table.

He sat and grabbed a fork and the container of potato salad. "I thought you were supposed to be some kind of crackerjack businesswoman. What possessed you to get involved with Mac Byrne?"

"Don't you think I checked him out first? I talked to a couple of people who've dealt with him. MacGowan Byrne is a well-known dealer—supposedly *reputable*—in art and collectibles. He locates pieces for well-heeled clients, for a commission. That's why I don't understand all this."

She settled on the mattress again. It felt good to cross her legs under the voluminous skirt and sit comfortably. Logan, his mouth full, tipped the potato salad toward her in offering. She shook her head and reached for her sandwich. It weighed several pounds.

She continued, "Mac first called a few weeks ago, on behalf of some mysterious, reclusive client. Some nut job willing to fork over beaucoup bucks for that worthless old ray gun of Mom's."

"A prop from *Return of the Atomic Bride*."

"Right. He called the apartment looking for Mom, but I answered the phone. Which seemed a stroke of luck at the time. If he'd talked to Mom, she'd never have agreed to part with the damn thing. He offered three grand at first. I mean, it was laughable. I could tell just by his tone of voice that whoever wanted that ray gun was willing to shell out a lot more than three grand."

"The infamous Zara Sutcliffe business savvy."

"I'm telling you, I could practically smell Mac's greed, even across the phone lines," she said, unwrapping her sandwich. "I've only spoken to him on the phone. Never met him in person. I don't even know what he looks like."

Something about the way Logan said, "I know,"

gave her pause. She glanced at him, but his expression revealed nothing.

He plunked the fork into the potato salad and set it on the table, then slid down a little on the rickety chair, crossing an ankle on his knee and lacing his fingers behind his head. She decided he was the type who could relax in any setting, no matter how austere.

His movements drew her attention to the sheer male elegance of his form. The shingled muscles of his abdomen tightened briefly under the snug T-shirt; his powerful thighs stressed the worn denim of his jeans.

Somehow she knew he was one of those rare big men with lightning-quick reflexes, a man gifted with speed and stamina as well as raw strength. She sensed it in the aura of confidence and authority he exuded, even in repose.

Nothing could get past him. No one could get to her while she was with him.

Which wasn't a wholly comforting thought.

Are you really an FBI agent?

If I'm not, it's a little too late for you to do anything about it now.

He eyed her sandwich with interest. "You gonna eat that?"

Forcing her attention to her meal, she took a bite. The mingled flavors and textures detonated in her mouth.

A groan of ecstasy erupted from her throat. A long, low moan of sheer gustatory rapture that warbled through a range of octaves. She couldn't help it. She'd always been absurdly appreciative of good food.

She shot an embarrassed glance at Logan, his indolent posture now at odds with the smoky intensity of his gaze. That's when she realized her shoulders had been doing that little shimmy she'd always thought of as her "yummy dance."

Suddenly she regretted her decision to shed her bra along with her stockings.

He leaned forward quickly. Drained half the tea in his bottle. "So. You upped the price."

Price? "Uh, yeah, I could tell when I was reaching the upper limit of what Mac's client was willing to pay. He was absurdly easy to read."

"Not so easy, as it turned out."

She stared at him.

He said, "If you could've read him for real, you'd have known he's a psychopath. A very dangerous psychopath."

She thought of her mother at the mercy of a homicidal maniac. She thought of Emma, timid, unprepossessing Emma, Daddy's "good girl," fending off a murder attempt.

All because of Zara's lapse in judgment. She and her sister had never been close, but still...

She was her twin. Her clone. The other half of herself.

Suddenly she couldn't swallow around a throat clogged with tears. She set down the sandwich and reiterated the questions he'd refused to answer during the drive from the airport. "You said he tried to kill her. What did he do? Was she hurt?"

He ignored her. "Didn't Mac's demands raise any alarms in your head? Didn't it occur to you, when he insisted on dealing only with you, that he might have something nasty planned?''

"Not really." She shrugged. "I just figured he was…eccentric. Like his clients. Like half the people I do business with in the New York publishing world and Hollywood. I figured I'd just meet him at his office in SoHo, like he asked, and exchange the ray gun for a certified check.''

"For two million bucks.''

The way he said it made her cringe at her own naïveté. Had she been so eager—no, desperate—for the cash that she'd ignored the signs of danger, relinquished her usual business savvy? Hell, her *common sense?*

For some reason, she wanted Logan to understand her motivations. "My mother has been living with me for the last two months, ever since her latest boyfriend dumped her and she had to move out of his houseboat. My divorce left me broke, Logan. I couldn't afford to buy or rent her anyplace decent.''

"Broke?'' His sneer of incredulity said it all as he treated her to an insolent once-over, his gaze lingering on her Movado watch.

She felt her face flame. "All my clothes and everything, that's all from before the divorce. I haven't bought anything new in a year and a half.'' Why did she feel compelled to explain herself to this arrogant, overbearing son of a bitch? "I sold all my jewelry. This is the only piece I kept.'' She indicated the watch.

"I'm ready to weep.''

"All I wanted was to set Mom up in a nice place of her own. You can't imagine what it's been like.

She's turned my beautiful apartment into a showcase for that disgusting collection of props from her horror flicks.''

The only halfway cool thing was the futuristic bride's dress on a mannequin—white satin, real short and ultra low-cut, with a big winglike collar and matching thigh-high boots. It was used in *The Atomic Bride.*

"I like those posters." He gestured dramatically. "*House of Blood,* in Bloodcolor! That one's my favorite. Though I gotta admit, that decapitated head under the glass dome—with all those electrodes?— that's pretty damn impressive."

Zara stared dumbly as her exhausted mind assimilated this latest development. "My God. You've been in my apartment. My home." Her precious sanctum. She felt violated. First her luggage, and now this. Her voice rose in pitch. "When? How did you get in? Did you paw through all my—my private things?"

"Relax. I'm one of the good guys, remember?"

Are you? She snapped her mouth shut, on the brink of verbalizing the question.

He smiled slowly. Reading her mind. "You know, I'd have thought you'd be more worried about your mother's welfare than whether I've been 'pawing' through your naughties. But since you brought it up. All that stuff—the lacy little bras and string panties, the garter belts and nighties and teddies, and those corset things…?" He jiggled his cupped hands under his pecs in illustration.

"*Bustiers.*" She forced the word through clenched teeth.

"All that stuff is from *before* the divorce?" He

chuckled. "Good old Tony. Guy must be a wild man."

She'd never thought of her ex in just that way, though she had to admit the description fit—utilizing a more literal definition of *wild*. Barbaric. Cruel. Malicious.

With Tony, she could never be certain where constructive criticism ended and pure spitefulness began. Some of it had to be true. After all, his recitation of her faults only echoed what she'd heard from her father's lips for so many years.

You're self-centered, Zara. Shallow. No moral fiber.

I'm ashamed to call you my daughter. Why can't you be more like Emma?

As for the "naughties," she wasn't surprised by Logan's testosterone-induced assumption that her husband had bought them for her. As if it were unheard-of for a woman to treat herself to pretty underthings for her own sake. As if the only function of such clothing were the sexual titillation of men.

He reached for a piece of carrot cake. She watched him unwrap it. Watched, transfixed, as his long, supple fingers slowly peeled back layers of cellophane. Finally he lifted the plastic wrap free and licked off the cream cheese frosting that adhered to it.

Zara swallowed, vaguely surprised when she didn't taste cream cheese frosting.

"So there you were," he said, wadding up the cellophane and lobbing it into a battered metal trash can, "all set to hand over the ray gun to your friendly neighborhood psycho, when things started falling apart down under on the set of some movie."

She nodded, grateful to occupy her mind with something besides Logan's tongue and her galloping imagination. "*Thunder in the Outback*. Maxine Moore is one of my clients." At his quizzical expression she said, "Maxine Moore, the novelist-screenwriter? *High and Mighty? Lake Forever?*"

"Never saw 'em."

"Well, anyway, Maxine's a tad temperamental when it comes to rewrites. Threw one of her patented hissy fits, and the next thing I know, everyone's suing everyone else. Two years of cutthroat negotiations to engineer this deal, and in two minutes she's got the whole thing going down the tubes. I had no choice. Had to fly out there right away and put out the brush fires, get the project back on track."

"So you made Emma pretend she was you to keep the appointment with Mac."

"I *asked* her to take my place. To borrow my clothes, impersonate me—a necessary subterfuge since Mac insisted—"

"I know. Insisted on dealing only with you."

Suddenly she felt deflated. Defeated. "There never was a certified check for two million dollars, was there?"

Logan shook his head.

Her eyes burned and she blinked to clear her vision. "He tried to kill Emma. He thought she was me and he tried to kill her."

He stared into the murky expanse of the warehouse. Those amber eyes lost their hard edge and appeared unfocused, troubled. "I think in the beginning he had every intention of going through with the sale," he said quietly. "A legitimate transaction."

She was catching on. "When he thought he could get the ray gun for a few grand."

"I figure his client's paying him a flat two mil, rather than a commission. The less money he has to pay you for the gun—"

"The more he gets to keep."

"Right. He wasn't prepared for you to jack up the price like that. In Mac Byrne's mind, shrewd business tactics and beautiful women occupy completely separate niches. He figured you'd jump at his initial offer—"

"And he'd be richer by nearly two million bucks." She hugged herself as a chill gripped her, though the room was warm. "Why did he try to kill me? I mean, why did he try to kill Emma when he thought she was me?"

"You can identify him by name. When he agreed to your price, it was a ruse. He planned to steal the ray gun and do you in so you couldn't finger him."

"Did he get away with the gun?"

"Not then, but eventually he got ahold of it. He doesn't give up easily."

"You're so sure of the guy. His motives, his plans, how his mind works. How can you be that sure, Logan?"

The terrain of his face shifted subtly, hardened. Zara hugged herself tighter.

"I know all about Mac Byrne," he said, at last. "I've been after him for months."

She knew the FBI had a Behavioral Science Unit that did criminal profiling. Was that the source of these insights?

She said, "So you met my plane and brought me

here just for my protection, to keep Mac away from me?"

Something flashed in his unguarded expression before he briefly turned away. Something that prickled the hairs on her nape.

But his voice was cool, with just a tinge of sarcasm. "I believe that's the point of a safe house."

"But you're also trying to apprehend Mac Byrne. And rescue my mother. Are the police involved?"

"No. Believe me, they'd only get in the way of an operation like this."

"So who's this Lou you were talking to? Another agent?"

He didn't answer. She felt invisible.

"What are you doing to locate my mother?"

"You know all you need to know, Zara."

She pounded the mattress in frustration. "Why are you keeping information from me? I have a right to know what happened while I was gone, what's being done to rescue Mom."

He rose and started stuffing the empty food wrappers in the paper sack.

She rose, too. "I will not be dismissed like some pesky child!" She grabbed his arm and got in his face. *"Where's my sister?"*

"I told you—she's safe."

"That's not good enough."

"It'll have to be. The less you know, the better."

"For who?"

Silence. She became aware of her nails gouging his arm where she gripped him. She uncurled her fingers and saw a row of red half-moons on his skin. He paid no notice.

"So that's it?" she asked, her voice tight. "I'm to be kept in the dark unless and until *you* decide there's something I need to know?"

"That's about the size of it."

She could have laughed if the circumstances weren't so dreadful. Here was renowned literary agent Zara Sutcliffe, a figure of immense power in New York and Hollywood, confined to a filthy, dilapidated warehouse, at the mercy of a man who might or might not be one of the good guys.

THE MAN WHO CALLED himself Logan Pierce watched Zara sleep. She lay curled up in one of his sleeping bags near the edge of the mattress, her rolled-up silk robe pillowing her head.

Around midnight he'd ordered her to hit the hay. She'd resisted, and he knew why. It wasn't easy to succumb to the vulnerability of sleep in the presence of someone you didn't trust. She was afraid of him. He knew that. He could have told her she had every reason to be.

In the end her acute exhaustion settled the matter. She'd been awake for more than twenty-four hours. Running on empty.

Rising, he unhooked his shoulder holster and dropped it on the battered steel desk. She flinched at the sound and he froze for a few seconds, until he heard her slow, rhythmic breathing once more. He extracted the Glock nine-millimeter and laid it on the floor at the head of his sleeping bag, next to the mattress. Slipped his T-shirt over his head and unbuckled his belt.

When she'd emerged from the bathroom after getting ready for bed, he hadn't known whether to laugh or jump her bones. He'd been all prepared to see her in some silky nothing of a nightie like the ones he'd found in her dresser drawers. Not this skimpy white tank-style undershirt that clung to every curve. The ribbed material stretched, and stretched some more, to accommodate high, full breasts, whose dusky tips he could just make out. If he tried hard enough.

And he certainly hadn't expected the black silk boxer shorts. Men's shorts. "Tony's?" he'd asked her. When he could find his voice.

"No," she'd answered, running coral-tipped fingers over the gleaming satin. "Women wear these now—they're comfortable."

Uh-huh. Maybe for her, but what they were doing to him was decidedly *un*comfortable, he mused, standing behind her as she knelt to lay out her sleeping bag.

She glanced over her shoulder and asked, "Where are you going to sleep?" A quivering hint of trepidation underscored the dry, don't-even-think-about-it tone.

She might be a big shot in business, all glitz and tough talk, but to him she was transparent as glass. His ability to size up people in a flash was a lifesaving skill he'd honed over the last fifteen years.

In his line of work, you needed every edge.

"I'm sleeping on the floor," he answered. "And I'm not that kind of boy, so don't get any ideas."

Her bug-eyed, slack-jawed response was entertaining for the second or two it lasted. Then one dark eyebrow rose and her mouth twisted into a devastating smirk—contemptuous, haughty, practiced—a smirk that had probably caused scores of hapless aspiring authors to wet themselves.

That article in *People* never mentioned that wide, provocative mouth. That piece on "Extra" didn't show her wriggling and moaning in orgasmic bliss as she devoured a Sicilian hero with everything on it. He'd done his homework, but it clearly wasn't enough.

Why did he have the feeling Zara Sutcliffe had a few more surprises in store for him?

He stripped off his jeans and turned off the light, then slid into his cold sleeping bag in nothing but his white briefs. He shifted onto his side and shoved the wadded-up jeans under his head, then slipped the Glock under the jeans for instant access. He didn't expect guests, but he knew that the day he let his guard down would probably be his last.

Zara's face was inches from his, slightly elevated because of the mattress. Little light reached them from the streetlamps five stories below; he could just make out her features. He wondered if she knew how innocent she appeared in sleep.

Her warm breath teased his eyelashes. Her scent wrapped around him, a lush, sensual blend of some expensive perfume and her own womanly essence. She smelled like night-blooming flowers, like illicit encounters in moonlit gazebos.

He reached up to brush wisps of dark hair off her cheek. Her skin felt like satin, bringing to mind those black boxer shorts. He remembered how the sleek fabric had hugged her bottom as she spread out her sleeping bag. How it had slid up a little, revealing the enticing underswells of a world-class butt.

He rolled onto his back and contemplated the painful arousal prodding his sleeping bag. At times like these he envied the fairer sex, whose libido, according to popular doctrine, was linked to emotional factors—issues of love, of trust and respect.

Whereas guys…well, guys were less complex.

He didn't trust or respect Zara Sutcliffe, and God knew he didn't love her. But she sure as hell turned him on. Which wasn't going to make what he had to do any easier.

He had to be careful. So far, she'd been fairly easy to control. But that would change in a heartbeat if she discovered who he really was—and that his plans for her had nothing to do with keeping her safe.

Chapter Three

Zara's eyes sprang open. Her heart slammed painfully, keeping time with the seesaw wail of a police siren outside, the sound at once far away and impossibly close.

She blinked into her dark surroundings. Nothing looked familiar. Where am I?

Don't panic.

She tried to sit but found herself immobilized, her body snared in a sacklike cocoon.

She panicked.

Disorientation magnified her terror as she twisted and clawed at the pillowy fabric encasing her, suffocating her. Her own breathless whimpers echoed off the walls of the huge empty room.

Fingers closed on her shoulder and she screamed. She fought the big, hot hand pushing her down, the solid pressure of a heavy arm across her chest, over what she now recognized as a sleeping bag.

"Shh, Zara...it's all right." A low voice, sleep-raspy.

She knew that voice. That voice meant...safety. Her terror and confusion gradually ebbed as fragments of the past day began to filter through, snapping together like pieces of a puzzle, forming a pattern her mind recognized.

Logan. Safe house. Mac Byrne.

The crushing sense of shame at her own culpability.

"Hang on a minute." He shifted off her and fumbled with the side of her bag nearest him. She heard the zipper open, felt the vibration down the side of her body, the cool air rushing in.

"That better?" His hand slipped inside her bag, over her midriff, still heaving as she struggled to calm her breathing. It felt weighty and substantial and immensely reassuring.

She nodded and offered a shaky "Yes." She could just make out his features in the semidark, his expression surprisingly intimate, almost compassionate.

Another side of this enigmatic man, or a dangerous illusion, a trick of the shadows and her own dark fears?

His long hair was loose now, falling around his face past his bare shoulders, making him appear barbarous, untamed. A few dark strands brushed her face. She'd forgotten how good a man could smell, the intoxicating essence of pure male animal underlying the civilized scents of soap and aftershave.

They stared at each other for a full minute, until her initial fear gave way to a different kind of turmoil. An uncomfortable awareness that played havoc with her slowing pulse, kicking up the tempo once more.

She knew he felt it, too, knew it by the subtle change in his breathing, the alertness of his gaze, the sudden tension radiating from his body into the hand still draped on her waist. His fingers moved, ever so slightly, and she stopped breathing.

He pulled back abruptly. Sat on his heels and dragged those long fingers through his hair, staring into the dark recesses of the warehouse.

She shivered, missing his heat, berating herself for her foolishness. She tucked the sleeping bag up under her chin. "Logan...?"

He looked at her.

"Do you think she's still alive? My mother?" *Don't shut me out,* she silently begged. *Please give me this one morsel of hope, something to hang on to.*

After a few moments he said carefully, "I have reason to believe Mac might not want to kill her."

She bit back a sob of relief. It wasn't a guarantee, but it was more than she'd had a minute ago. She knew not to ask for specifics. "Thank you," she rasped.

He frowned, studying her intently. Finally he said, "Get some sleep, Zara." He slid into his sleeping bag, his back to her.

WILLIAM KEPT his expression neutral, his tone of voice bland, as he addressed his associate across the wide expanse of his black marble desk. "You've been very enterprising."

Mac Byrne shrugged lazily, drumming his fingers on his crossed knee. "What can I tell you? I'm always one step ahead, anticipating my clients' needs."

"Yes. Well." William leaned forward. Mac mimicked the posture. "This takes our arrangement to a whole nother plane, doesn't it?"

Mac raised his palms in unspoken concurrence. His

eyes shone with an unholy mixture of greed and something William was beginning to suspect was madness.

He had to proceed carefully.

"Where are you keeping her?" he asked.

Mac leaned back with a cagey smile. "Leave the particulars to me. That's what you pay me for."

William's jaw clenched. "Yes. So it is."

"Speaking of which…" Mac indicated the solitary object lying on the desktop: Candy Carmelle's ray gun. "We'll settle up on this now, get it out of the way."

William tapped his lips with his steepled index fingers. "No. No, I don't think so."

Mac's eyes widened.

"I prefer a package deal. The gun and Candy. One price for both."

Mac's Adam's apple bobbed. "That wasn't the agreement."

William smiled grimly. "Neither was kidnapping. Seems I underestimated your initiative. What are your terms?"

Mac licked his lips. "Ten million."

"Four."

Mac made a rude noise. "Eight. That's my final offer, and I deserve every penny of it. I'm taking a hell of a risk here, William. She can identify me. I might have to go into hiding, change my name." He tried to stare William down but was the first to blink.

"I don't have it."

"Bull."

"Not liquid, I mean. It would take a couple of weeks, minimum, to get ahold of that kind of cash."

Mac slapped the arm of his chair. "Lean on someone, dammit! I'm not gonna wait two weeks."

William asked, "And if I fail to come up with the money? For argument's sake," he added quickly. "What happens to Candy then?"

Mac's tone of voice was downright guileless. "She becomes a very sad story on page five, William." His sweeping gesture indicated the headline. "Former Starlet Found Drowned—Drug Use Suspected." He snickered. "She'll learn what it really means to be washed up."

The image Mac's words conjured was too painful to contemplate. "That won't be necessary. I'm a man of my word. You just make sure nothing happens to her."

"*You* just make sure I get my eight mil. Pronto." He slouched in his chair, a cocky smile in place.

"I want to see her. I want to see for myself that she's unharmed."

"Sorry. You'll have to take my word on that."

William knew better than to take this maniac's word on anything, but at the moment he had no choice. "Listen. About her being able to identify you. Don't give it a thought. Once she realizes what a sweet deal she has with me, she'll kiss you in gratitude. Turning you in will be the last thing on her mind."

"You sound pretty sure of yourself. Must be this obsession of yours, all those Candy souvenirs you've been collecting for decades. The photos, news clippings." He nodded toward the ray gun. "Relics from her film career. You might've convinced yourself you know what makes the lady tick, but the truth is, she doesn't know you from Adam, am I right?''

Something in his sly eyes, the way he said it, put William on the alert. Mac was fishing. This was dangerous territory.

"That's true, of course, but the fact is, I can be very persuasive. Have you forgotten she's spent the last three years living in some dilapidated houseboat? Until Easter, that is.''

Mac looked around, taking in the sumptuous furnishings of William's East Coast office. "You got a point. I can't see her squawking once you install her in that mansion of yours out in Hollywood.''

"And unless I miss my guess, the daughter doesn't want her living with her anymore. The literary agent. Zara.''

At that, Mac's expression turned chillingly flat, his pupils mere pinpoints. His fingers tightened on the arm of his chair. William wondered what it was about Zara Sutcliffe that triggered such a reaction.

His mind raced. "Zara wasn't home when you grabbed Candy, was she? You didn't have to... subdue her...?''

"No. She was overseas, on business.''

William let out the breath he was holding. He didn't ask how Mac had managed to purchase the ray gun from Zara while she was out of the country. He'd had enough of the man's smarmy evasiveness.

He stood. "Give me a number where I can reach you.''

"Can't do that, but I'll call you every day. Around noon.'' He rose, too. "Get moving on the money, William. Light a fire under someone.''

William didn't offer his hand. "I will be very displeased if anything happens to Candy." He spoke slowly and deliberately. "Need I tell you, I possess the resources to more than even the score when something displeases me." He watched Mac's face go rigid.

"Are you threatening me?"

"Yes." He smiled thinly. "I'm glad we understand each other. Close the door on your way out."

"DON'T LIE TO ME. I know he's been in touch with you." Logan stared at Madeline Byrne's stiff back as she stirred a pot on the stove. The mouth-watering aroma of spicy chili permeated the entire house.

She opened the oven door and checked the golden corn bread swelling in a cast-iron pan. "You'll believe what you want to believe, no matter what we say."

Douglas Byrne spoke from the doorway of the shabby little kitchen. "If I'd known you were here to harass us, I wouldn't have let you in."

He sighed. "Look, I know this isn't easy for you."

"You don't know a damn thing!" Douglas stalked toward him. "What right do you have barging in here demanding answers!"

Madeline turned around, her face drawn. "Douglas…"

"I want him out of here!"

Logan held his ground. He knew they'd go to any lengths to protect Mac. "When was the last time you saw him?"

Madeline's faded blue eyes glistened; her mouth quivered. In that moment Logan didn't know who he despised more, Mac or himself. "You don't get it, do you?'' she whispered. "You actually expect us to betray our own son.''

"Careful, Maddie,'' Douglas sneered. "Anything you say can and will be used against you. Isn't that how it works, *Agent* Byrne?''

Logan stood there staring at his father, absorbing his contempt. "I quit the FBI two years ago. You know that.''

"Then why the hell can't you leave your brother alone? What is this…*vendetta* you have? Do you hate Mac that much?''

I don't hate my brother, I love him, he wanted to say. *God help me, I still love him.*

"This isn't about hate. He's hurting people, Dad. He's hurting *himself.* It's just a matter of time before he crosses the line and does something…''

Something he's already planned. He thought of Zara Sutcliffe swaddled in her sleeping bag, trembling under his touch, her brown eyes wide and liquid in the semidark.

He blinked away the unwelcome image. "When that day comes—and it will if no one stops him— then God help him. God help us all. There'll be no saving him then. Have you forgotten New York State now has a death penalty?''

Their stricken expressions caused a brief flare of hope that he'd gotten through to them at last.

He should have known better. His mother recovered first, approaching him slowly, hesitantly, as if he were a stranger to be feared. He felt something in his chest wrench painfully. Even after everything, the horror and heartache of the last two decades, this distance between them, the soul-deep sense of loss, still tore at him.

She stopped directly in front of him, her face a mask of anguish and outrage. "Where's your sense of loyalty? Don't you know what it means to stick by your family? Are you that cold? I look at you and I wonder what kind of man I've raised." Tears spilled from her eyes and traced the creases of her weary face.

Logan lifted his hands…and dropped them at his sides without touching her. "I know you think you're helping Mac, Mom, but you're hurting him. Every time you lie for him, every time you take him in and shield him from the authorities, you're making it worse."

"He's different!" she shrieked, gesturing wildly, her face mottled. "He's not like you. You can take care of yourself. Mac needs our help—"

"I'm trying to help him!"

His father shouted, "By hauling him to jail?"

"Mac won't go to prison. He belongs in a mental facility. He's brain damaged."

"Don't say that," Madeline wailed. "He's not…like that. He's just different. Ever since the accident."

Logan didn't bother reminding her that the event that irrevocably altered the life of an eighteen-year-old Mac Byrne was no accident.

He said, "Mac has kidnapped a woman."

His parents recoiled as if he'd struck them. Douglas said, "That's a lie!"

"A sixty-one-year-old woman with two daughters who are worried sick about her." He watched his parents exchange uneasy glances. "I don't know where he's keeping her," he continued. "If you have any idea at all where he might be hiding out..."

His father shook his head mutely. They both avoided Logan's eyes. "I don't believe it," Douglas muttered.

Logan's parents appeared frail, exhausted by the hardships of their life, not the least of which was loving a son like MacGowan Byrne. They'd bought this modest little house in Orange County, New York, thirty-five years ago, when their twin sons were happy, dark-haired infants and the future glowed with limitless potential.

He wondered if they lay in bed at night sharing memories of those halcyon days, wishing they could turn back the clock.

He moved to the wall phone and the message board mounted next to it. A marker dangled from a string. "Here's my phone number. It's a cellular phone, but it's always on. Call me if anything occurs to you. Anything."

His mother glanced at the number quickly, almost furtively, as if he'd inscribed an obscene limerick on the wall of her kitchen. He wondered if she'd erase it the minute he left.

They didn't ask him to stay for lunch. He let himself out quietly, thinking about how much his brother loved chili and corn bread.

"RUN THIS BY ME AGAIN. Why exactly do I have to do this?" Zara's palm perspired around the small cellular phone.

"You're my best bet to draw Mac out of hiding."

"Because he has nasty things in store for me." She tried to smile.

Something close to understanding flickered in Logan's eyes. He didn't respond but simply pried her stiff, cold fingers from around the phone and flipped it open. "You won't have to talk to him, Zara. You'll get his answering machine. He's been careful to avoid his home and office. This is the only way to get in touch with him." He punched in some numbers. "I'd do it myself if I could."

He handed her the phone. She told herself she was being ridiculous. She didn't have to face the guy—she didn't even have to talk directly to him. All she had to do was force her voice to remain calm and—

"You have reached the office of MacGowan Byrne Ltd." It was a brisk female voice. "Leave a message and your call will be returned as soon as possible."

As she waited for the beep, Zara forced a couple of deep breaths and pretended this nightmare wasn't real, that the recipient of her message wasn't out for her blood. Logan was betting that Mac didn't know Zara was on to him. With any luck, he'd think Zara had just gotten back into town and didn't know about her mother's kidnapping or the meeting that nearly ended in Emma's death.

Beep.

"Mac, this is Zara Sutcliffe. I was wondering if it would be possible for you to meet me this evening—I've just acquired a couple of pieces of Hollywood memorabilia that I think you might be interested in."

Logan gestured at her. *Slow down.* Another deep breath.

"You won't be able to reach me this afternoon, but

I'm hoping you get this message in time to meet me at Vincenza's in Little Italy. Say, eight o'clock? See you then."

She snapped the phone closed, squeezed her eyes shut and groaned, feeling her pulse sprint. Logan's warm, clean scent filled her nostrils and she inhaled deeply, comforted by his proximity. Only when she felt his hand on the back of her head did she realize she'd slumped against him. She opened her eyes and they homed in on the black grip of his semiautomatic resting in his holster, inches from her face.

Her head whipped up and she scuttled back a step.

"You did great," he said.

"I did? Do you think so? Do you think he'll get the message in time?"

"I know he will. Mac checks his machine several times a day."

She was about to ask how he knew a detail like that before she remembered that he'd already danced around that question once.

She'd woken early, as soon as the sun had lit the huge warehouse room. The space next to her on the floor had been empty. No sleeping bag. No Logan.

Had she dreamed that strange interlude in the middle of the night? His deep, gentle voice, his hand on her waist. The startling sense of intimacy.

She'd looked around and found his sleeping bag, neatly rolled and placed with the luggage. She'd risen and stretched, listening for sounds from the bathroom. Nothing.

Had he left her again? She'd crossed the cold concrete floor and verified that the john was vacant. When she tried the door through which she'd entered the warehouse, she saw that, once more, she was locked in. The dead bolt needed a key from either side.

He said it was for her protection, but still it rankled. Special Agent Logan Pierce was entirely too autocratic for her taste.

Apparently he'd made an early morning breakfast run—she found a sack of bagels, still warm, a container of cream cheese, a bottle of orange juice and a large cardboard cup of coffee, plus several packets of sugar, diet sweetener and half-and-half. Eagerly tugging the lid off the coffee, she mused that that file at FBI headquarters must not include the fact that she took her coffee black.

As she ate half a poppy-seed bagel with the thinnest *schmeer* of cream cheese—had the man never heard of low fat?—she eyed his duffel. The day before, when he'd deposited her like so much baggage and left for three hours, she hadn't had the nerve to take a peek.

Now she was a half day wearier, a few degrees less intimidated and a whole hell of a lot more frustrated. And that duffel was just too tantalizing.

Besides, hadn't this man unapologetically searched not only her luggage but her *home*, as well?

The less you know, the better.

"Oh, I don't think so," she murmured, and abandoned her breakfast to saunter across the room to Agent Pierce's bag.

Rationally she knew he'd never leave anything important lying around where she could prowl through it. Still, she admitted to a certain curiosity about the man himself—the taciturn G-man with the hard golden eyes. Her irrepressible imagination again.

She approached the big, scraped-up canvas duffel as if it might explode at the first touch. No lock. She grasped the zipper pull and glanced at the door. And opened the duffel all the way until it lay gaping before her.

She bent down to peer inside, afraid to touch anything. She saw T-shirts, underwear and socks, jeans, rugged work shoes, a dark hooded sweatshirt and a plastic garbage bag, apparently for dirty laundry. Shoving the clothing aside, she spied a few small cartons. Bullets. Well, no surprise there. And a leather contraption, which she soon identified as a small holster, the kind that could be concealed beneath a waistband.

A worn leather toilet kit was tucked at the end. She lifted it out and shook it, hearing small objects rattle around. She'd seen his toothbrush, soap and razor on the rim of the rust-stained sink in the bathroom, a small bottle of shampoo in the cramped, mildewy shower stall. She unzipped the kit and poked at the contents. A couple of extra disposable shavers, odds and ends like Band-Aids and Q-Tips.

She smiled, tickled by the ludicrous notion of traveling with a toilet kit this size. She herself needed separate bulky bags for her makeup, toiletries and hair-care appliances. Not to mention her portable iron and lighted makeup mirror.

Her fingers brushed against something with a sharp corner. She pulled it out and stood staring at a string of condom packets. Half a dozen of them.

"Oh my." Lubricated. Ultrasensitive. She peered at the fine print. *Ribbed for her pleasure.*

The thought of Agent Pierce ribbed for her pleasure sprang into her consciousness before she could shoot it down. When she could breathe again she carefully refolded the packets, accordion-style, and replaced them in the kit. She chewed her lip. Was that just where they were before? Would he notice she'd been through it? Would he care?

Oh, God.

She'd shoved the kit back in the duffel and yanked the thing closed with a vengeance. And turned to her own luggage to find something to wear.

He'd returned in the early afternoon, with yet more food. Did he think if he kept her stomach filled, she wouldn't notice she was a virtual prisoner?

Now, watching him kneel by his open duffel, inspecting the contents, she felt her heart squirm into her throat. His back was to her, and she watched the play of powerful muscles beneath his navy T-shirt. She heard the whisper of a zipper and knew he was looking in his toilet kit.

Just whose damn pleasure were those things ribbed for, anyway? Was there some wife or lady friend somewhere, or did Logan carry the things around in case he got lucky?

He threw a glance over his shoulder. "Been going through my stuff, Zara?"

Her throat tried to close, but she managed to squeak, "No! God, no!" She didn't know why she was embarrassed. He'd felt no compunction about pawing through *her* worldly possessions.

He stared at her a moment, expressionless. He

knew. He turned back to his duffel and zipped it. "Just don't mess with the ammo."

Her face was on fire. She'd never get one up on the man. Taking a deep breath, she said, "I want a key to this place."

"No." He stood and faced her, as implacable as ever.

She stalked up to him. "Come on, Logan. I've been cooped up in this—" she glanced at her dingy surroundings "—'safe house' for twenty-four hours. I'm bouncing off the walls. I don't have my work, which must be a mountain on my desk by now. I don't have any books to read or—or even a newspaper." Just her own inventive imagination—not the best companion for her peace of mind at the moment.

"You want a magazine or something, I'll pick it up when I go—"

"I want out of here! O-u-t!" She pointed to the door.

"Look, I know this isn't the Plaza, I know you're bored and frustrated, but I can't have you traipsing all—"

"Give me a little credit. What do you think I'm going to do, stand in the middle of Park Avenue wearing a bull's-eye around my neck?"

"It would be extremely dangerous for you to go *anywhere* alone."

"I'm not planning any excursions. I just can't stand being locked in here like I'm some kind of prisoner. I'll bet you have a second key to that dead bolt."

His gaze flicked to the lock in question for a moment as he pondered her request. Finally he shoved his hand in his jeans pocket and produced a key ring.

Zara let out the breath she'd been holding. She held out her palm and he dropped a brass key in it.

His voice was gruff. "In case the place goes up in flames while I'm gone. Don't even think about stepping foot outside that door unless I'm with you."

"I appreciate this," she said, knowing it wasn't easy for him to relinquish total command over the situation and trust her even this much. Deciding to press her luck, she said, "Let me go with you when you check out the restaurant."

"Out of the question. I'm not going there to pick up takeout, I'm trying to flush a dangerous criminal out of hiding. If he takes the bait and shows up..."

He didn't have to say it. She'd only be in the way. Might even be in danger. Zara hadn't stamped her foot since she was about six, but she was sorely tempted now.

She asked, "How do you know Mac isn't lurking around my apartment or my office, looking for me, even as we speak? You can't be in two places at once."

She recognized that obdurate expression. Incommunicado.

"So you have associates," she said. "People working for you. Or with you. Like your pal Lou. Funny. I had you figured for a loner. The type who doesn't like to rely on anyone else."

That got to him, she could tell. Did he think he was the only perceptive one?

She continued, "I have to be able to size people up in my business, too, Logan." Or maybe a part of her simply recognized a kindred spirit.

He crossed his arms over his chest. "If you're so

good at sizing up people, maybe you've made up your mind. Am I one of the good guys?''

She pondered that seriously, thought about everything she'd learned about Logan Pierce in their brief time together. He was aloof, sure, and arrogant as hell. But something in the way he talked about Mac Byrne told her he was sincere. A cold obsession underlay his mission to bring Mac to justice. What had caused that obsession, she couldn't guess, but she knew one thing: she wouldn't want to be in Mac Byrne's shoes.

"Yes," she said. "You're one of the good guys."

"Do you believe I know what I'm doing?"

"Yes."

"Then don't question me when I tell you how things have to be. This isn't some game we're playing, Zara. Your mother's life is in danger, in case you've forgotten."

She sucked in a deep breath. "As if I could." She knew what he was thinking. That she was shallow, selfish. It was the same message that had been drummed into her her whole life. Maybe it was true. Look at the tragedy her actions had reaped.

Her eyes burned and she turned to stare out the window. She didn't have her freedom or her peace of mind. At least she could try to hold on to her pride.

He was silent a long while. Finally he said quietly, "Where would you like to go?"

She spun to look at him, certain she must have misheard.

"Mac won't be looking for you anywhere but your usual haunts. I guess it wouldn't hurt for you to get out and clear the cobwebs. As long as you're with me. Don't even think about going out on your own."

His thunderous expression reinforced the warning. He grabbed his lightweight windbreaker and shrugged into it, zipping the bottom few inches to keep his gun concealed. "But after this, I don't want to hear any more whining. Got it?"

She grabbed her purse, giddy with anticipation. "Got it." She slipped into a pair of crimson pumps that matched her short linen sheath dress, and retrieved her heavy silk jewelry roll from her Pullman bag. "Just a sec." She could no more venture into public unaccessorized than she could negotiate multimillion-dollar deals in her bathrobe.

Logan watched her sort through her trinkets. "I thought you said you sold all your jewelry."

"I did. This stuff's all costume." She found the earrings she'd been hunting for and waggled them at him. "Five bucks on the sidewalk in Chinatown. What do you think?" The silver earrings were adorned with ponderous, dangling red and black glass beads. The ear wires were extra long, eliminating the need for hooks or clasps. She slid them into her pierced ears. "I'm ready."

Logan frowned, studying her ears. He slowly approached her.

She said, "You don't like them?"

He stopped scant inches in front of her and lifted his hand to the left earring. She heard the beads clink together, felt his fingertips graze her neck. His touch was so gentle, she felt dizzy.

"They're heavy," he murmured, staring at the beads.

She didn't trust herself to speak.

"Don't they hurt?"

"No," she managed to whisper.

He carefully pulled on the long wire, withdrawing it from her earlobe with excruciating slowness.

The world fell away. Nothing existed but that one pinpoint of sensation where the silver filament slid through her flesh.

When it was free he studied the glittering gewgaw, peering at it as if it could tell him something about its wearer. It looked incongruous nestled in his huge palm.

At length he brought it to her ear again. When she realized he meant to replace it himself, she started, on the verge of objecting. But instead she stood paralyzed as he gently grasped her earlobe and touched the end of the wire to it.

She swallowed hard. His eyes were riveted to his task, which he approached with absorption. She nearly flinched when she felt the wire penetrate. He pushed it through as slowly and meticulously as he'd removed it. When he was done, every nerve in her body hummed. He flicked the beads and watched them dance, and met her eyes at last.

"Let's go."

Chapter Four

"I haven't been here in years." Zara stared up at the full-scale model of a blue whale that hung suspended over her head in a diving pose. This replica had fascinated her as a child. She couldn't imagine any animal being that huge. Nearly the length of the enormous exhibit hall, it had small, glassy eyes and white spots on its flanks.

"I come here a lot," Logan said, gazing around the huge, dimly lit Ocean Life and Biology of Fishes hall, a popular exhibit at the Museum of Natural History.

The room was two stories high. A walkway circled the upper level, which featured educational displays in glass cases, above which hung life-size replicas of sharks, stingrays and swordfish in lighted niches. Zara and Logan were on the lower level, where dioramas of marine animals in their natural habitats were set along the perimeter. Each life-size display was behind glass, backlit and painstakingly detailed.

Zara's father had brought her and Emma to the museum once when they were seven. She remembered that trip vividly. She'd returned a couple of times in the years she'd lived in New York, and each time she felt the same childlike wonder.

During that visit with her father, Zara had been on her best behavior—or tried to be. As usual, he'd found abundant reasons to chastise her. *Don't touch the dinosaur skeleton, Zara. Slow down and wait for your sister, Zara. Keep your voice down, Zara.*

When she grew to adulthood and learned the term *control freak,* she began to gain a better perspective on John Sutcliffe. She wondered if she'd ever understand the man who had sired her and Emma. How could family members be so different? He was five years in his grave and still she heard his imperious voice cataloging her shortcomings, felt his sharp, condemning glare at the most inopportune moments.

"We can leave," Logan said.

She snapped out of her reverie. "What?"

"You don't look exactly thrilled to be here."

"I am. Trust me. I was just thinking…" She faltered and he raised his eyebrows. "I was thinking about my father."

"Seals and walruses remind you of your father?"

"Maybe that fellow." She nodded toward a display of a polar bear, fangs bared. On the ice floe near it was a dead ribbon seal, with blood flowing from its mouth.

Logan said, "He was strict?"

"You could say that. Emma never had trouble living up to his expectations. But me…well, after a while I think it just kind of turned into this self-fulfilling prophesy. I knew nothing I did would please him, so why bother trying? And, too, I found the more outrageous I was, the more I got to him. I think he was the reason I drove myself so hard to succeed careerwise. That was something he respected, I knew. Money. Success. But even that wasn't enough.''

"Is that why you and your sister ended up different? Your father's warped ideas about child rearing?"

"I guess so.'' Why was she opening up to him like this? ''What else could cause twins to develop such distinct personalities except the way they were raised? Nurture versus nature and all that.''

After a moment Logan said, ''Other factors have been known to come into play.'' He was staring at the bear's menacing fangs, the soft light from the diorama highlighting his strong features.

"Like what?"

He was silent so long, she thought he hadn't heard her. Finally he said, ''Chemical imbalances. Brain damage. That sort of thing.''

"Oh. Sure, I guess so. That doesn't apply to Emma and me, though. Thank God. Do you have any brothers or sisters?"

His eyes had been focused on the bear. Now they found her reflection in the glass. ''No.''

He started walking again, and they slowly made the circuit past the giant octopus, the pearl divers, sea otters and dolphins, toward the stairs leading to the second level and the exit.

He said, ''It must've been rough for your father to raise two kids alone. After Candy left him.''

"He left our day-to-day care in the hands of nannies. His involvement extended to lectures on behavior and character development. And as for Mom, you should hear her side of the story. I grew up thinking she'd abandoned us—that's what Dad told us.''

"That must've been rough.''

"When he died five years ago, Emma and I tracked Mom down. By that time we both knew what an overbearing son of a bitch our father had been. When Mom told us how he'd ruthlessly wrested custody from her, we believed her. It was in character.''

"Guy sounds like a gem. At least you had your sister.''

She sighed. "Emma and I were never close. Even as children. I...I'm not proud of that. Dad was always comparing us, always pitting us against each other, and of course, I always fell short. But I can't lay all the blame on him. I'm not an impressionable child anymore, I'm a grown woman. I could've tried harder to undo the damage, to...make up for lost time with Emma. To...I don't know...'' Her throat tightened. "To get to know her, I guess.'' She met his eyes. "But I've always loved her, Logan.''

"It works both ways. She could've made the effort, too.'' They walked side by side up the steps.

"Things are going to change between us. I'll make sure of that. When this whole mess is over, I'm going to do whatever I have to, to make it right with her. If anything happens to Emma—'' She choked on the words, her tears too close to the surface.

Logan grabbed her elbow and pulled her to one side of the exit. He glanced into the distance a moment as if battling his impulses. "Do you remember scheduling an appointment with Gage Foster?''

Her mind flipped over, trying to absorb the abrupt

change in subject. "Gage Foster? The novelist? What about him?"

"You were supposed to meet with him, but you got called away to Australia. Does any of this ring a bell?"

"Well, sure. I've been after Foster for months. Me and every other agent in this city. Have you read *Incision?*"

"Yep."

"What did you think?"

"Damn good medical thriller."

Her excitement over the prospect of adding this *New York Times* bestselling author to her list momentarily eclipsed her worries for Emma and Candy. "I've been wild to bring Foster on board with my agency. Pleaded with him to come up from Arkansas to talk about it. Then this thing with Maxine Moore came up and I had my secretary, Tina, cancel the appointment. Now I'll have to reschedule and hope he—"

"Tina didn't call him in time. Foster flew up for the meeting."

"What? But I wasn't there!"

"No, but Emma was."

"Emma?" Her head throbbed with the effort of following this convoluted discussion.

"He showed up at your office as planned—"

"Oh, God."

"—and so did Emma."

"Wearing my clothes. For the meeting with Mac, when she had to pretend to be me. I asked her to go to my office to pick up the ray gun. Don't tell me. Gage Foster thought she was me."

"It's a long story. Maybe you'll read about it in his next book. The point is, if it weren't for Foster, Emma wouldn't be alive."

"He—he saved her life?"

Logan held up a hand, forestalling the volley of questions poised to leap off her tongue. "I just thought you'd want to know she wasn't alone, that she had an ally. *Has* an ally."

"Has?"

Logan smiled, a slow, revealing grin.

"They hit it off? Gage and Emma? I don't believe it." Shy, unprepossessing Emma and a wealthy, semi-reclusive, hunky surgeon-turned-novelist? The man Zara thought of as the Golden Cowboy?

"Believe it. She'll have a hell of a tale to tell when you see her next."

She shook her head in wonder. "Why are you being so forthcoming all of a sudden? Why are you telling me all this?"

He scowled. "I shouldn't. The less you know—"

"Don't say it. Just one more question. Is Gage still in New York? Is he staying with Emma at her place in Queens?" One look at his face told her she'd gotten as much out of him as she could. For the moment. She paused, collecting her thoughts. "Thanks, Logan. It makes it easier, knowing she didn't have to face...whatever she faced...alone."

He sighed. Regretting his revelations? No matter. She knew more now than she did five minutes ago. Not only about Emma's situation, but about Logan, as well. Despite the well-honed aura of surly inflexibility, he was human after all.

She couldn't help wondering what had made him

the way he was. What had his childhood been like? Why had he joined the FBI? And the question foremost in her mind: why was he so fixated on apprehending Mac Byrne? It wasn't what he said so much as the look in his eye. He was close to this case—too close? Was his judgment affected? Could his zeal put her in danger?

Wordlessly he placed his palm on the small of her back and steered her through the exit into the Invertebrates hall. From there they passed through the main lobby and into the North American Mammals exhibit.

Here, too, the models were set against ultrarealistic backdrops, complete with foliage and other natural elements. It was easy to imagine these deer, bison and caribou as live animals in the wild.

They made their way through the hall and down a side corridor past coyotes and skunks. Zara stopped dead at the next display. Here two wolves sprinted across a snow-covered landscape. They were posed in midleap, frozen in a lethal lunge toward the glass— toward *her*.

The exhibit was eerily dim, a twilight scene that held her spellbound. She couldn't make out the animals' eye color in the gloom, or the teeth. Nevertheless, it was all too easy to imagine herself some hapless woodland creature transfixed by two pairs of pale, predatory eyes, by the sight of bared fangs going for her jugular.

She sensed a third pair of wolf eyes on her.

"We have to be getting back," he murmured, his breath fluttering her hair. "I need to get to Vincenza's well before eight."

She dragged her gaze from the exhibit, breaking the spell. "Do you think he'll show?"

"I sure as hell hope so. And if you want to get your life back anytime soon, you'd better hope so, too."

HE DIDN'T SHOW.

Logan had selected Vincenza's because, together, he and Lou could effectively, and discreetly, surveil the restaurant and its immediate environs.

Perhaps Mac had suspected a trap. Perhaps he, too, had been out there somewhere, watching the front door, waiting for Zara to arrive.

Logan stayed a couple of hours, till it was clear his quarry had eluded him. Just as he'd waited in vain yesterday after leaving his parents' home, certain they'd expected Mac for lunch. A sense of unreality had suffused him as he found an unobtrusive spot down the block to observe the house. Was he really doing this? Staking out his childhood home?

What kind of man have I raised? his mother wanted to know. *The kind of man who spied on his own flesh and blood, on the people who gave him life and raised him,* he could have answered, sickened that their misguided sense of duty had driven him to it.

He suspected that as soon as Logan left, they'd called Mac and warned him to stay away.

After unlocking the chain-link fence and parking the BMW near the warehouse's loading bay, Logan let himself into the building he laughably called a "safe house" and rode the creaky old freight elevator to the fifth floor. He unlocked the door, questioning his sanity for giving Zara a key. How in the hell had she managed that one?

Movement drew his eye to the middle of the room. Zara was exercising, using a sleeping bag as a mat. She was dressed in skintight purple bike shorts and one of those little sports bras that doubled as a gym top. Canary yellow. She was doing crunches, lying on her back with her fingers linked under her head, raising her shoulders and bent legs together.

He watched her abdominal muscles tighten with each rhythmic crunch, her breath coming in sharp puffs. Her skin glistened and her short hair was spiky with sweat. She lay back on the sleeping bag a few moments, panting, then gracefully rolled up to sit cross-legged. She grabbed the hand towel she'd placed nearby and wiped her face.

"He didn't show," she said. It wasn't a question.

"No." In seconds he was out of both his windbreaker and his holster. He tossed them on the desk and sprawled on the bare mattress. The shade of the nearby floor lamp was tipped toward the wall, so his eyes were spared.

"What do we do now?" she asked.

You don't want to know.

He turned his head and stared at her sitting there in the shadows, her eyes big and dark and trusting. *You brought me here for my protection, right?* she'd asked him. He hadn't denied it.

His plan had made sense days ago, before he'd met the lady. Now, somehow, the idea of using her that way seemed a lot less palatable.

She said, "Maybe…maybe there's something I can do. Some way I can help."

Was she thinking along the same lines he was? Was the offer sincere? He doubted it. This wasn't the type of woman who willingly placed herself in harm's way, for any reason. Not a spoiled, self-absorbed fashion plate like Zara Sutcliffe. This type of woman was accustomed to having other people do her dirty work for her. People like Logan Byrne. With that in mind, he couldn't help baiting her.

"Like what, Zara?" He rolled onto his side, propped his head on a hand. "How do you figure on helping out?"

She didn't answer. Probably trying to find a way to weasel out of her halfhearted offer. Good luck. When the time came, she'd have to be involved, despite her reservations—and his. He just hoped he could count on her to keep her head.

He said, "Do you usually exercise at night?"

"No, in the mornings. But I was nervous, waiting for you to come back, wondering what happened. Couldn't keep my mind on the novel I was reading." They'd purchased a few paperbacks and magazines on their way back from the museum. "So I decided to give myself a good workout."

"Did it help?"

"No." She came to her feet. "I'm going to go shower off."

The next minute he lay there listening to the muted sounds of the needle spray pelting fiberglass. The sound shifted, and he pictured Zara moving around in the shower stall, soaping up. She probably had to contort herself a bit in that tiny stall, as he had, to get thoroughly clean.

Was she rinsing off now? Running her hands over her body, making sure she got all the soap off?

Cleanliness is next to horniness.

"You're pathetic, Byrne," he growled. He'd never even been attracted to polished corporate types like Zara Sutcliffe. Must be those naughty undies she wore. When you knew that underneath a woman's don't-mess-with-me power suit you'd find a half-cup see-through push-up bra and matching garter belt, your interest couldn't help but be piqued.

Along with other things. Logan contemplated his bulging fly with disgust. "This isn't part of the game plan," he told his erection. "Settle down."

The shower stopped and his mind's eye pictured her toweling off, carefully drying every nook and cranny. A half minute later the bathroom door opened and he rolled onto his stomach with a muttered curse, resting his head on his folded arms.

He heard her quietly replacing items in her luggage, then nothing. The light touch of her hand on his back made him flinch.

"I thought you might be asleep," she murmured.

He felt her sit next to him, felt her soap-and-shampoo-scented warmth. Turning his head, he saw she was wearing a black tank top and orange satin boxers.

"You look like Halloween."

"Not the fashion statement I was aiming for."

He reached over and plucked the slippery satin. "How many colors do you have these in?"

"How many colors are there?"

He smiled, deciding he liked satin boxers on women. On this woman at least.

She half turned to bend and look him in the eye. "I'm serious, Logan. What's the next step? How are we going to find my mother?"

"Here's what I want you to do." How much should he tell her? "You're going to call Mac's machine again. Apologize for missing the meeting and reschedule. Something came up."

"Will he believe that?"

"Probably not. He might figure you're on to him, maybe even that you've contacted the police."

"I've been thinking that might not be such a bad idea."

"The cops?"

She nodded.

He rolled to his side and propped himself on an elbow, comfortably flaccid once more. "Listen to me, Zara. If Mac suspects the police are involved, he might just snap."

"And hurt my mother."

"Yes."

"But you said he doesn't want to kill her."

"I don't think he does, but you've gotta understand, the guy's unstable. Unpredictable. Anything can put him over the edge."

"He won't show up to meet me if he thinks I'm on to him."

Logan chose his words carefully. "He might, with the right incentive."

"What would that be?"

"We'll discuss that when the time comes."

"I feel so helpless, sitting around here while Mom is God knows where, at the mercy of that..." She sighed raggedly.

"Something tells me Candy Carmelle can hold her own."

"She's spunky, it's true. Streetwise. But..."

He heard the catch in her voice. His hand automatically settled on hers. Her wet hair was combed back, but some strands fell on her forehead. He pushed them back and she met his eyes, her own shiny. He sensed she held herself together with an effort.

Whatever else he might think of her, she wasn't devoid of feeling. As much as he hated to admit it, there was more to Zara Sutcliffe than the one-dimensional business shark profiled in the media. This lady was no caricature.

Her voice was hoarse. "I don't fall apart easily. I mean, it takes a lot. I can put up with...well, practically anything if it's in normal doses." A watery chuckle. "But when the stress just keeps up, with no end in sight...well, I feel like I'm going to crack."

Her candidness moved him.

She said, "That's how it was with my divorce. It was...ugly. And it dragged on so long. Tony was so damn vicious, so greedy." She took a deep breath, not meeting his eyes. "I want to be strong, Logan. I want to help you, not hinder you. I just hope..." She shrugged helplessly. "I just hope I can. For Mom."

He held her quivering chin and made her look at him. "I'll help you get through it," he murmured, and smiled gently. "You help me and I'll help you. Deal?"

Her eyes brimmed. She looked about twelve. "Deal," she whispered.

He leaned toward her without intending to and

touched his lips to hers. He felt a little shock course through her. He knew he should move back, break this kiss, which had started as a token of comfort, but he couldn't. Her eyes closed and overflowed at last, twin tears trailing down her cheeks.

He relinquished her soft lips and pressed his mouth to the glistening track of a tear. His hand caressed the back of her neck, damp from the wet ends of her hair.

Logan didn't hear her soft breaths, but he felt them, fanning his cheek, his ear. Felt her breasts brush his chest in the same agitated rhythm. His hand slid down her back to press her to him, to trap her softness against him.

He claimed her mouth again, harder, fiercer, the warnings of his rational mind a faint whisper under the roaring din of his hunger. He opened her, sought her tongue, explored her mouth in a ruthless possession. She stiffened, and instinctively he intensified the kiss, nudging the answering passion he sensed within her.

Pressing her into the mattress, he angled his body over hers. She gasped and wrenched her head aside, her nails like talons through his T-shirt. He barely heard her breathless "No!"

Logan went still. He muttered a curse, rolled off her and got to his feet, putting some distance between them. She sat up shakily and wrapped her arms around her knees. She was ashen, avoiding his eyes, prompting him to replay the last few moments in his mind. His gut knotted. What did she think he was going to do—force her?

After a hellish silence he said, "That wasn't supposed to happen."

She said nothing, just tightened her grip on her knees.

"It won't, again."

She nodded stiffly.

He blew out a sharp breath and shook his head at his own folly, his loss of control. He crossed to an open window and filled his lungs, tried to chase away the lingering fog of desire. He said, "This is a…an awkward arrangement we have here, Zara, the two of us cooped up together. Hopefully it won't be for long. Meanwhile, let's just…keep our distance."

No reply.

"Will you say something?" he barked.

"Agreed." It was a hoarse whisper. Her eyes flicked to him, then away. She opened her mouth to say something, but didn't.

"All right, then," he said.

He laid out his sleeping bag—near the windows, a good fifteen feet from the mattress—and fled the building for a long, solitary walk. He returned an hour and a half later to find the lights still on and Zara sound asleep in her bag, clutching a book, a psychological thriller that had just come out in paperback. He smiled, imagining the valiant battle she must have waged to keep her eyes open.

He got ready for bed and crawled into his own bag, as jumpy as when he'd walked out, resigned to lying awake most of the night. He envied Zara the oblivion of sleep.

Chapter Five

Candy stared at the ceiling of her basement prison, tracking the sound of Mac's pacing one flight overhead. Whenever the footfalls reached the wall, they paused for a few moments, and she imagined him gazing out a window. Was it nice outside? No light made it past the plywood boarding up the basement window.

Mac was talking on the phone, she could tell. Once in a while some loud exclamation made it to her ears. She glanced around, not entirely sure what she was looking for. She went into the small laundry room and scanned the assortment of household detritus piled near the furnace.

In seconds she was back in the main room, dragging a straight chair near the wall. She stepped up on it and lifted her find, a three-foot section of PVC piping. She pressed one end to the ceiling—the undersides of the upstairs floorboards. She nearly toppled contorting herself to angle her ear to the other end. But it paid off.

"...have a deal, William!"

Who's William?

"Save your threats," Mac snarled. "Trying to live up to your name, huh? You wanna play hardball, I'll show you hardball. Your precious Candy Carmelle with two little Xs for eyes."

Candy felt a wave of icy dread even as she asked herself, *Whose* precious Candy Carmelle? Who could he be talking to? Only Emma and Zara would care about her fate. Could William be the mysterious "cowboy" who'd given Mac such a walloping? Somehow she doubted it. Her side was beginning to cramp from her awkward position.

"Then keep your end of the bargain. Two days, William. You've got two days to get me the money."

Candy swallowed hard.

A long pause. "Four, then. Exactly ninety-six hours from now I better be eight million dollars richer or she's dead."

Eight million! She nearly lost her footing on the chair. Who did she know with eight million dollars!

He said, "I'll be in touch." Immediately his heavy footfalls cut a path to the basement door. Candy leapt from the chair and shoved the pipe under the sofa as the key scraped and the door flew open.

Mac pounded down the steps and stopped short when he saw her. She knew she was flushed, breathing hard. His eyes narrowed.

"Aerobics," she said, jogging in place as if she were cooling down. "High impact. You oughta try it."

His gaze homed in on her body, bouncingly displayed in his own short terry cloth bathrobe. She could see the internal struggle; he didn't want to find a woman a quarter century older than himself attractive.

Touch luck, she thought. She was still a hot item.

"Where are your clothes?" he asked.

"Washer. I took a sponge bath at the utility sink, but I didn't want to put my dirty things back on. I found this in the dryer. Didn't think you'd mind. You don't mind, do you, Mac?"

He didn't respond, just lifted the tray with her empty breakfast dishes and disappeared upstairs.

"WHY CAN'T I just *talk* to her?"

"Why can't you just trust my judgment?" Logan slid his gun into his shoulder holster and picked up his windbreaker.

"Because she's my sister!"

"I thought you realized I know what I'm doing, Zara. Don't you think I have reasons for my decisions? Or do you think I get my rocks off playing the tyrant?"

"Maybe."

He threw up his hands. "Why the hell am I explaining myself to you? You'll talk to Emma when this whole thing blows over. Not a minute sooner."

She trailed him to the desk, where he'd left his keys and phone. "Where are you going?"

Surly silence greeted this query.

"When will you be back?"

"Tonight's bowling league, remember, dear? Keep the meat loaf warm and kiss the kids good-night for me."

She leveled what she hoped was a withering glare,

even as her face warmed. He was right, damn him, she *did* sound like some shrewish housewife!

He slipped his slim little cellular phone in a pocket of his windbreaker. How she wished he'd get careless and leave it behind! He wagged a finger at her. "Remember, don't open the door for anyone."

"I won't, dear," she said in cloying tones. "Oh, and don't forget to take out the garbage, *precious*." She grabbed the paper sack containing the remains of their dinner—Chinese takeout—and tossed it at him. Hard. Grinning, he caught it one-handed, unlocked the door and was gone.

She moved to the windows and stood staring down on the quiet street. It was 8:00 p.m. on Sunday, and this industrial neighborhood was nearly deserted. The sky was a bruised purplish hue, and the long shadows in the warehouse had given way to a pervasive gloom. But she didn't want to turn on the light just yet. The dark was where her deepest thoughts dwelled. She could corral them better on their home turf.

That afternoon she'd left another message on Mac Byrne's answering machine, apologizing for missing their meeting at Vincenza's and promising to call the next day to reschedule.

She hoped she'd sounded convincing, but she was so bleary and exhausted, it was hard to judge. After Logan had stepped out last night, she'd drifted off while reading, only to be booted awake by a chilling dream in which her parents argued about her and Emma. Dad, bombastic and cruel; Mom, tearful, pleading.

Candy had left them when she and Emma were just over a year old. Could this dream be some deep-seated memory or just a cruel trick of her overtaxed mind?

She'd fallen asleep with the light on but woke up with it off. Squinting into the gloom, she'd made out the hump of Logan's sleeping bag under the windows. She'd found solace in his presence, just knowing she wasn't alone.

Once she was awake, further sleep had eluded her. Her mind had raced, her roller-coaster imagination conjuring one horrific scenario after another. Her only consolation had been in knowing she wasn't the only sleepless one. Logan's restless shifting and irregular breathing had given him away.

Ironically, that wretched night had preceded a pleasant, even serene, day. She and Logan had spent the morning chatting and noshing and reading the Sunday *New York Times* like some old married couple. She'd told him much more about herself than she ever meant to. Despite his often rigid demeanor, there was something about him that invited confidences, impelled her to open up. As different as they were, she sensed a kindred spirit.

She'd told him about her upbringing at the hands of John Sutcliffe, remembered things she'd long forgotten, painful incidents she'd managed to bury beneath the slick veneer she presented to the outside world. It had been a catharsis, sharing some of that. She'd come away with one inescapable truth, something she'd been reluctant to acknowledge: her father had been an unrivaled son of a bitch.

He'd raised his daughters in an inflexible environment of strict discipline and emotional manipulation. He'd wrested custody of Emma and Zara from their mother, not for the girls' sake, but because Candy had had the temerity to leave him. His daughters had become spoils of war. It hadn't mattered that Candy had been a good mother. It hadn't mattered that her babies needed her.

In the end, John Sutcliffe had controlled everything and everyone around him. Had he died happy?

God help her, she hoped not.

She'd told Logan about her unhappy marriage. Not all of it—there were some things she'd never speak of.

But the rest she'd shared with him during that long, lazy day, and in his understated way he'd seemed interested. He'd asked leading questions and actually listened to the answers.

Naturally she'd asked him about his own life. What had his childhood been like? How had he gotten involved with the FBI? He'd neatly dodged most of her questions, but in so doing revealed more about himself than she thought he meant to. She'd detected traces of the man within, even in his evasions. Anguish, pride, betrayal. They were all there.

She'd been left with the conviction that she and Logan were connected on some level. He was a loner, and in her own way, so was she. She'd learned the hard way never to rely on anyone else for emotional fulfillment. Everyone she'd ever trusted with her tender feelings had let her down: father, sister, husband, even her mother, though not by choice. As far as she was concerned, she was on her own for the duration.

Logan had embraced that particular sentiment with

a telling enthusiasm. *Never trust anyone,* he'd said, *and you won't be disappointed.*

Zara stood at the window and watched him emerge onto the sidewalk. Even from five stories up, he was impressive, with his wide shoulders and powerful, long-legged stride.

He looked up as he passed, directly at her. Had he known she was watching? Had he sensed her eyes on him? A funny little smile crossed his face before he disappeared from view.

You'll talk to Emma when this whole thing blows over. Not a minute sooner.

Arrogant man. What possible reason could he have for forbidding her to communicate with her sister? She just wanted to assure herself she was okay, as he claimed. A reasonable request.

A tiny voice inside whispered, *He's afraid of what Emma might tell you. Afraid of what you might learn about the case—or perhaps about Logan himself.*

Zara only had his word that Emma was safe. If she'd been hurt…or worse…was it possible he'd conceal that from her? He was charged with protecting her, keeping her here at this safe house. He had to know that if she suspected Emma needed her, she'd be anything but docile and easy to manage, as she had been the last two days.

The more she thought about it, the more her suspicions blossomed, though she had a hard time reconciling that brand of duplicity with the complex, haunted man she was beginning to know. Still, she refused to kid herself. He had a job to do. She had no doubt that he was capable of manipulating the truth, if it made that job easier.

She looked up and down the block. Only when she spotted it did she realize what she'd been looking for.

The telephone booth beckoned like the pot of gold at the end of a rainbow. Two minutes and a quarter could buy her peace of mind. She had the phone number for Emma's new house in Queens in her address book.

She moved quickly. Zara Sutcliffe hadn't gotten where she was by being indecisive. That was her sister's specialty. She chose not to dwell on the fact that she'd promised Logan she wouldn't leave the building without him. Well, that wasn't entirely accurate. He'd *ordered* her not to leave. A little smile tugged at her lips. She didn't recall promising anything.

She rode the big, rickety elevator to the first floor and let herself out of the building, alert for any sign of danger. In the glow of the streetlights she saw only one other person, an unkempt man swaying on his feet, muttering to himself and gesticulating with a bottle wrapped in a brown bag.

She made it to the end of the block in seconds, but it seemed like the longest trek of her life.

Damn Agent Pierce for making her paranoid in her own beloved city.

She reached the phone booth, if the abbreviated version in use nowadays could be called a booth. She fished her address book out of her purse and dropped a quarter in the slot. After one ring a recording kicked in, in a voice eerily similar to her own. She'd never gotten used to that.

"You have reached 555-6439. I'm sorry I cannot come to the phone right now..."

Zara rolled her eyes. Her first order of business would be to help her staid twin sister jazz up her message.

"If you leave your name and phone number at the tone, I'll return your call as soon as possible."

Zara waited impatiently for the beep.

"Emma, it's Zara. Dammit, I wish you were home. I got into town on Friday. Seems all hell broke loose while I was gone. I just need...I need to talk to you. You can't reach me. I'll try calling back later...."

She squeezed her eyes shut, appalled by the prospect of slinking back up to that warehouse with nothing to show for this defiant excursion.

"Listen, I'll—I'll be there soon. At your place. It's, uh—" she checked her watch "—eight-twenty now. I should be there within about forty-five minutes. Okay? If you get in, sit tight!"

She replaced the receiver. She must be nuts. What if Logan returned while she was gone? She had no idea how long he'd be out.

The hell with him, she decided. Hadn't he forced her to take matters into her own hands with his "Me Tarzan" routine?

Knowing few taxis would be cruising this side street at this hour, she hurried to Tenth Avenue and bolted into the street to snag the first vacant cab she spied.

The ride to Queens was interminable. She'd never been to Emma's new home. At first she thought the cabbie had brought her to the wrong place. But no, the address was right. It was a one-story brick-and-frame bungalow with a tiny, weedy lawn and a rusted chain-link fence. No lights on. Emma wasn't home yet.

"Wait here," she told the driver, hoping she could find a way to get into the house. She tried the front door and found it unlocked. She groaned at her sister's trusting spirit. "You aren't in the wilds of Maine anymore, Emma. You're a New Yorker now, you'll have to learn to lock up." Still, she was grateful, just this once, for Emma's naïveté.

Zara paid the driver and sent him on his way, then let herself into the hovel her sister called home. She couldn't see much in the dark, and she groped for a light switch.

When she flicked it on, her own horrified gasp broke the silence. The place had been torn apart. "Oh, my God..." she whimpered as she took in the disarray that had once been a living room. Furniture upended, bookcases toppled, spewing enough beat-up paperbacks to carpet the floor.

Had Emma been home when the place was broken into? If so, where was she now?

Common sense dictated she leave immediately. The intruder might still be in the house. But for all she knew, her sister could be here, too, hurt or unconscious. Needing her help. She had to look.

She scanned the place for a weapon and came up with a pair of sewing shears lying amid a jumble of craft supplies. Gingerly she picked her way through the mess.

Emma had obviously been in the midst of unpacking from her move. Meticulously labeled cartons were strewn around, spilling their contents: Nonfiction, A-G. Mysteries, H-P. A bark of hysterical laughter burst from her. Her sister still arranged her books by the author's last name. She'd always loved whodunits.

A carton labeled *CraftWorld* lay upended near a mound of magazines. Emma had written freelance craft articles for the publication until its recent demise had forced her to take a staff writing position with *Crafty Lady* magazine here in New York. Hence the move from Maine to Queens. She knew Emma relished the independence of freelance work and had dreaded the new in-house job, but financial considerations had forced her to accept it.

Even amid the horror of the devastation surrounding her, she couldn't help noticing the squalid furnishings and tacky wallpaper. Had they come with the place or had Emma actually *selected* them? She thought of her own luxurious penthouse apartment on East Eighty-sixth Street in Manhattan. How long would she last in a dump like this?

Then again, she thought, slogging through the chaos to the rooms beyond, she herself now called a grubby, roach-infested warehouse home. She had to admit, Emma's green-flocked wallpaper looked downright swanky by comparison.

She toured the tiny, antiquated kitchen, the utilitarian bathroom and the two bedrooms, one of which Emma obviously planned to turn into an office. They, too, had been ransacked.

Her fears were unfounded. No bogeyman leapt from the shadows. The place was deserted.

"Emma, where are you, honey?" she breathed, tossing the scissors on her sister's nightstand. "*Where are you?*" She'd meant what she'd said to Logan. When this whole thing blew over, she was going to pull out the stops and heal her relationship with her sister. The one good thing to come out of this debacle with Mac Byrne was the realigning of her priorities.

She thought about the popular idea that identical twins shared a sort of telepathy, that they could sense what was happening to each other. Fanciful nonsense, yet how she wished it were true at this moment.

She straightened the mattress, which had been stripped and yanked half off the bed. Unspeakably weary, she kicked off her shoes and plopped on it, stretching full length. Would she ever again know the luxury of sheets?

Her sleepless night was catching up to her. That and nerves. She stared at the old-fashioned light fixture glowing overhead, a milky glass dish through which she counted seven fly corpses. It wouldn't hurt to rest awhile, she reasoned. As soon as she had her second wind, she'd call a taxi and return to her glamorous home away from home before Logan even knew she'd stepped out.

HE INVADED HER DREAM, with his flagrant male hunger. His carnal fury. Whipping a tempest of raw, scorching need with no release.

And she wasn't afraid. Not this time.

She fought the tug of wakefulness, wanting—needing—this dream. Needing him any way she could have him.

Hands on her, urgent, possessive, stroking her through her clothes.

"Open your eyes, Zara."

She did.

A scream barreled out of her throat, arrested by the big palm clamped over her mouth.

"Easy."

The light had been turned off. In the dark she could barely see him, a shadow looming over her. But it was *his* voice. It was *his* long, silky hair tickling her face. His hand felt strange against her lips, the skin too smooth. He slowly removed it.

"Logan," she breathed. "I…" She almost said, *I was dreaming about you.*

No. She couldn't tell him that.

"How—how did you know I was here?"

He nuzzled her throat, and she gasped. "You can't hide from me, Zara. That was careless, leaving a message on Emma's machine."

Belatedly she realized her sister must have given Logan the remote code to retrieve her messages. His hand swept over her body. Instinct drew her arms up, a flimsy barrier between them. Last night he'd said this wouldn't happen again. *Let's just keep our distance.*

"Logan, don't—"

He silenced her with his mouth. His hand found her breast and squeezed it through her silk blouse. He ignored her muffled protests, her attempt to dislodge his grasping fingers. The more she struggled, the more aggressive he became, until she found herself pinned beneath him. His mouth was voracious. This wasn't the impassioned kiss of last night—this was a taking, not a sharing.

Her anger surged, lending her strength. She twisted beneath him, bringing elbows and knees into play. *"I said stop!"*

She cried out in pain as he seized her forearms roughly and slammed them on the mattress near her ears. His mouth ground against hers, cruelly.

Some part of her—some primal animal part—didn't recognize this man. Her senses were in discord, sending conflicting messages to her brain. Something was different. The scent of him, the taste of him...

Relying on instinct, she bit his lip savagely, and he jerked back with a bellow of outrage. His hand arced up to strike her and she turned away, taking the blow on the back of the head.

Pain lanced her skull, momentarily stunning her.

One of the good guys, she dully thought. Logan was supposed to be one of the good guys.

He rose off the bed, but somehow she knew he wasn't finished with her. She heard him leave the room. She sat up and swung her legs over the side of the bed, fighting dizziness, forcing her mind into problem-solving mode.

The scissors. She'd dropped them on the nightstand. She groped in the dark and came up with nothing more lethal than a clock radio.

She squinted against the sudden glare of the overhead light.

"A precaution," he said, leaning against the door frame, swinging the shears from one long finger. Now she saw why his hand had felt odd—latex gloves. The kind surgeons wear. The kind criminals wear when they don't want to leave fingerprints. He flung the scissors into a corner.

Her gut clenched. She'd never seen that taunting smile before. "Logan." She gained her feet. "Why are you doing this?"

"Wish we had more time." He pushed off the door frame. "I'd give you one hell of a ride. Take these."

Only then did she notice what else he was holding. A paper bathroom cup and a prescription vial. He shook out the contents—six small white pills.

"What is that?" Her voice wobbled.

"Painkillers. Heavy-duty stuff, too."

"Those are Emma's?"

"Yep." Logan examined the prescription label. "Couple of years old. Probably had a tooth out or something. Guess she didn't need them all." He tossed the vial. "Take 'em."

"No." Her knees were shaking.

Logan drew his gun from under his waistband. That's when she realized he'd changed clothes. The teal raw silk shirt and beige linen slacks were a far cry from the weathered gray polo shirt and jeans he'd worn earlier. The ponytail was gone, his long hair brushed back off his face, revealing the edge of a scar at his hairline that she'd never noticed before.

Those little changes made an amazing difference in his appearance—though the biggest difference of all was his expression. Glacial. As if the two of them hadn't spent half the day sprawled on the mattress in the warehouse, the Sunday *Times* spread out around them, rolling in muffin crumbs and empty coffee cups, working the crossword puzzle and reading the editorials to each other. As if she hadn't revealed more of herself to him than she had to anyone, ever.

"Logan," she breathed. "You don't want to do this." Whatever he had in mind, she knew *she* didn't want him to do it.

He slowly approached her. His implacable golden

stare held her immobile, bringing to mind once more that picture of a wolf in her father's den. Ruthless. Single-minded. The quintessential predator.

Casually he touched the barrel of the gun to her chest. "I prefer not to shoot you. But I will if I have to."

She felt the blood drain from her head as she accepted the cup of water. He dropped the pills into her hand.

"I wish I could've found more," he said. "That would make it easier on you. Easier on both of us."

His words squeezed her stomach like a fist. She wondered giddily if she'd be able to get the pills down her tight throat—and keep them down.

He watched as she placed them in her mouth and chased them with a swallow of water.

He said, "Open up."

She endured the humiliating exercise of opening her mouth to prove she wasn't hiding the pills.

Satisfied, he gestured with the gun. "Strip."

The soft-spoken word paralyzed her. *This isn't happening,* she told herself. *Logan isn't doing this to me.*

"Logan—"

Without warning, he tore open her blouse, sending buttons flying. "Hurry up." He stalked to the pile of clothes tossed from Emma's dresser drawers and kicked aside sweaters, underwear and socks until he found what he was looking for—a swimsuit. A plain black one-piece with a demure neckline. What Zara thought of as a "grandma suit."

He tossed it at her. "Put it on."

She forced herself to undress as Logan stood

watching. "Emma isn't really safe, is she? You—you did something to her."

She couldn't sort it all out. If Logan was working for Mac Byrne, if he'd never intended to let her live, why had he tucked her away in a warehouse off Tenth Avenue for two days? Murderers didn't feed their victims Sicilian heroes and mu shu pork and take them to the museum when they whined about cabin fever.

He stared fixedly as she dropped her blouse and stepped out of the short leather skirt. For the first time in her life, she wished she wore sedate white cotton undies like Emma.

"You and your old lady," he said, with a little head shake. "You sure know how to show off what you've got."

She presented her back and quickly divested herself of garter belt, stockings and bra. She whipped off the panties and pulled on the swimsuit in about three seconds.

"That wasn't so hard, was it?" he snickered.

She'd kill him, she thought, turning around to face him. If he gave her half a chance, she'd wring the bastard's neck. Tears scalded her eyes, less from humiliation than from a profound sense of betrayal.

This man had made her feel something. She'd exposed her bleeding soul to him, her insecurities and yearnings, the hurts of her past and her prayers for the future. For his part, he'd shown an underlying gentleness, a vulnerability she'd suspected the rest of the world never got to see. Either he was a consummate actor or she was a first-class fool.

She'd even felt an exhilarating sexual longing for the first time since well before her divorce: a stunning resurrection of that which her ex-husband had methodically obliterated.

He'd made her feel that, damn him, this animal now pointing a gun at her!

He gestured toward the doorway. "How about a little nightcap?"

Chafing the gooseflesh on her arms, she preceded him into the living room. He righted a tattered easy chair and ordered her to sit. Already she was feeling woozy. The rump-sprung cushions were a welcome support, saving her the bothersome chore of keeping her feet under her. She wished she had more in her stomach to slow down the drug. She'd eaten a light dinner, knowing that if she kept letting Logan stuff her with food, she'd soon need a larger wardrobe.

She watched, a little too placidly, she knew, as he entered the kitchen. She heard him crunching over the broken glass that littered the tile floor, heard the refrigerator door open. By the time her muddled mind decided to make a run for it, he was back, a half-filled bottle of white wine in hand.

"Thirsty?" he cheerfully asked, holstering his gun.

"Does it matter?"

"I'm afraid not." He pulled the cork and held the bottle out to her. "Bottoms up."

"I don't drink Chablis." Her tongue got in the way of the words.

"I'm a martini man myself. Drink." He wagged the bottle.

She stared languidly at the golden liquid sloshing in the bottle. "Don't I get a glass?"

Logan sat on the arm of the chair, facing her. He tilted her chin, studied her eyes. "Ladies and gentlemen, we have reached cruising altitude." He slipped a palm behind her head to hold her steady as he tipped the bottle to her lips.

She resisted briefly, but too soon the woolly part of her mind, the part that wanted nothing more than to curl up and take a nap, won out. The cold wine went down like acid. She coughed and sputtered and he gave her a respite.

"Okay?" he asked after a moment, and wiped her chin with his gloved fingers. His expression, his tone of voice, were solicitous.

She nodded.

He brought the bottle to her lips several more times, until it was empty, until her eyes drooped and he had to prop her up with an arm around her shoulders.

"Come on, Zara. Time for a swim." He pulled her up and she slumped against him.

She giggled. "I'm too drunk to go swimming."

"That's the point."

She staggered with him through the disheveled house toward the back door. A corner of her mind was aware that the next few moments would be critical to her existence. Her life hung in the balance, but she couldn't rouse herself to do anything about it.

He said, "Life has become too much for you, Zara. Your failed marriage. Your money problems. Your strained relationship with your sister. She was always Daddy's favorite. You never were able to please him, were you?"

"You're a good listener," she mumbled, and tripped over the remains of a potted spider plant. He steadied her.

"These things have you very depressed," he said. "You've decided the pain isn't worth it. You've given up."

"No I haven't," she said.

"Yes." He opened the back door. "You have."

She planted her feet and they both skidded to a halt in the doorway. The cool night breeze arrowed through the fuzz in her brain to impart one last moment of lucidity. "You're going to kill me, aren't you? And make it look like I killed myself."

He shrugged. "Could be seen as an accidental drowning, too. Too much booze, too many pills. Watch your step, now." He guided her out the door, over the cracked cement patio and the small patch of lawn.

"I thought you were one of the good guys. I'm very disappointed in you, Logan."

She felt the vibrations of his harsh chuckle in the arm supporting her. "Imagine that," he mused. "Logan Byrne disappointing someone."

Byrne? Didn't he know his own name?

"Now, Logan's brother..." He shook his head regretfully. "Talk about a disappointment. Definitely not one of your good guys, Zara."

"You don't have a brother."

"I'm working on it."

In the dark she could just make out a tall stockade fence running the perimeter of the property, and in the center, an aboveground pool taking up most of the small yard. It was oblong, about five feet deep and eighteen feet long.

He stood still a moment, listening, alert for nosy neighbors, she assumed, though the tall fence afforded privacy. He looked down at her. "Not much farther. How're you holding up?"

"Okay," she said on a yawn.

At the pool, he boosted her up the aluminum ladder and followed her. She stood unsteadily on the metal deck perched over one end of the pool. The water looked inky, silver moonlight spilling over the tranquil surface.

She had to lean against Logan for support, his warmth a shocking contrast to the cool night air. She shivered.

He whispered in her ear, "In you go."

Sweet unconsciousness beckoned. She struggled to stay awake, to engage her mind, to recall where this bizarre scenario was leading.

She said, "Nobody will believe I killed myself, Logan. I'm a fighter, I don't give up."

"You're a fighter? Let's see you fight."

The icy water jolted her brain. She hadn't felt him push her, and now his strong hands held her under. Her frenzied mind and starved lungs screamed for air, but her body was sluggish, unresponsive.

The fight left her too soon. The last thing she saw was Logan's face through the veil of water, those pale, dispassionate eyes watching her die.

Chapter Six

The lights were on. Logan knew then that his hunch had paid off. He'd suspected as much, after her shrill insistence on talking to Emma.

He pulled into the driveway and hopped out of the BMW. His first order of business would be relieving her of the key to the warehouse. He smiled grimly, recalling his earlier words. *Never trust anyone and you won't be disappointed.* How he wished he'd heeded his own advice.

He pounded on the door. "Zara! Open up!"

He didn't wait but immediately tried the door. Unlocked. *Figures.*

Did the woman have no inkling of the danger she was in? Hadn't he made it clear enough?

A cold ball of anxiety settled in his stomach.

No, he had to admit. He hadn't made it as clear as he could have. He'd chosen to keep her in the dark about certain details; hell, about almost everything. He had his reasons, but right now, as he contemplated the peril Zara had placed herself in, those reasons didn't seem quite so compelling.

He let himself into Emma's house and again surveyed the damage Mac had done days ago, searching for Candy's ray gun.

"Zara!"

Nothing.

"Don't hide from me. I'm going to find you." *And when I do, you'll wish I hadn't.*

Swiftly he searched the small house. Could she have stepped out? There were no stores within walking distance. He noticed the empty bottle of Chablis on the floor of the living room. The fact that it was standing upright told him it had been set there after Mac ransacked the house.

"Have yourself a little party for one, Zara?" he murmured, though he couldn't picture her sitting here getting quietly sozzled. She had other things on her mind—namely, her sister's safety. He knew she must have been frantic at finding Emma's home in this condition.

He could have told Zara exactly where Emma was, but that would have complicated matters, made her more difficult to handle. If she spoke to her sister, she'd find out about Logan's connection to Mac Byrne. He recalled how suspicious she'd been of him in the beginning. Once she found out he was the twin brother of the man who wanted her dead, he wouldn't have a prayer of securing her cooperation.

At least that's what he'd told himself. He hadn't counted on Zara Sutcliffe—by all accounts shallow and self-absorbed—caring enough about her semiestranged sister to defy him like this and put herself at risk. He'd underestimated her level of frustration, and her devotion to Emma.

Where could she be?

One place remained to be checked.

He opened the back door. "Zara!"

A sudden movement in the moonlit backyard drew his attention. His legs started moving before his rational mind assimilated what he'd seen.

His own startled eyes staring back at him.

Mac turned and leapt over the pool railing onto the lawn like some great lithe beast.

Logan had him! After four long months of obsessive pursuit. Four months of waking each morning wondering if he was too late, if his brother had already crossed the line beyond which there would be no helping him.

The worst four months of Logan's life. And here was Mac at last, within his grasp!

As he rounded the pool he spotted him clambering up the fence. Logan actually grinned, anticipating the next few seconds: the short sprint to the fence, the gut-deep satisfaction he was sure to feel as he dragged his brother to the grass and subdued him.

Mac couldn't get away from him. Not this time.

Something teased at the edge of his vision as he swung around the pool. Something pale on the murky surface of the water.

His churning legs stopped, stumbled. A sick wave of dread overwhelmed him. He knew before he looked.

Zara.

It wasn't too late to catch Mac. But at what cost? Seconds counted for a drowning victim. He had an impossible choice to make, but some part of him, some fathomless, primordial part, took the decision out of his hands.

He bounded up the pool ladder even as Mac hoisted himself over the fence. Zara was floating facedown, making barely a ripple on the surface of the pool. He knelt on the deck and leaned out over the water, grasping her cool ankle.

He hauled her up onto the deck, where she lay limp and unresponsive. He tilted her head back and put his ear close to her mouth, hoping for a ripple of air, the rise and fall of her chest.

Nothing.

But she had a pulse. Barely. Placing his fingertips on her throat, he detected the faint ticking of her carotid artery.

Not allowing another second to lapse, he pinched her nostrils and sealed his mouth over hers, delivering four fast full breaths as a start.

You're not going to die, he silently vowed.

He continued breathing for her every five seconds, waiting, praying for her own lungs to take over.

Minutes passed.

"Breathe, damn you!" he growled between puffs. "I will not lose you, Zara. *Breathe!*"

She lay deathly still. There was no way to tell how long Mac had held her under. Logan never considered stopping the resuscitation. He'd keep it up as long as it took.

Time seemed suspended. It could have been ten minutes or an hour. At last a faint gurgle sounded from her throat.

"That's it, honey. Come on."

He delivered another breath, and another.

A rattling cough shook her and he gently turned her on her side, facing him. Water poured from her lungs. She groaned pitifully, her eyes still closed. He squeezed his own eyes shut for a moment against the storm of unfamiliar emotions assailing him.

He kept talking, soothingly, as he gently lifted her and carried her down the ladder. "You're going to be all right, Zara. It's over. You're okay."

Her labored breathing sounded beautiful to his ears. Shudders racked her. The first order of business was to get her warm and dry.

He carried her in his arms across the lawn. "Come on, honey. Open your eyes for me."

She blinked, straining to focus on his face. With recognition came terror. She cried out, flailing weakly against his hold.

He stopped in his tracks. "Zara, it's me. Logan."

Her struggles increased. She writhed and struck out at him, depleting her meager strength. He lowered her to the cool grass and held her, turning her face to his.

"Look at me, Zara. He's gone. It's Logan."

Her panicked eyes raked his face; they took in his hair tied back in a ponytail, his gray polo shirt.

"See? It's me." His fingers lightly stroked her cheek. She shrank from his touch. She looked impossibly pale in the moonlight, her eyes huge and dark and eloquent. He read confusion, betrayal.

And then he knew.

He pretended to be me. He let her think I was doing this to her. In that instant he was glad he hadn't caught Mac. He'd have killed him on the spot.

She pushed on his arms and he let her slide out of his embrace. Keeping him in her sights, she scuttled back, then turned and crawled a few shaky feet. She stopped, doubled over, retching violently. He was at her side in an instant.

She whirled away from him. "Don't touch me!"

He sat on his heels, his heart breaking. "Please. Listen to me. I didn't do this to you, Zara. I'll explain it all, but I have to get you inside first. You're in shock."

This time he didn't let her fend him off. He seized her quickly and scooped her into his arms. She collapsed, exhausted, the fight gone out of her. Her breathing was fast and shallow. He held her close to try to still her shivering, but it didn't help.

"You'll be warm soon, I promise."

He let himself into the house and strode through the debris to the bedroom. Under the bright light her pallor was frightening, those lush lips blue. Her eyes were open, glazed. He lowered her to the bare mattress and swiftly pulled the sodden swimsuit off her. Under any other circumstances he'd have lingered to appreciate the view, but at the moment voyeurism was the last thing on his mind.

He lifted a quilt from the floor and swaddled her in it, then quickly grabbed a towel from the bathroom and rubbed her scalp. Her dark hair stood out in spiky tufts, and he smoothed it down.

He rubbed her arms through the quilt. "Zara." His tone was gentle, undemanding. "Did he make you drink that wine?"

Her gaze homed in on his face. He saw confusion, but her fear seemed to have abated. "Wine. And...and pills."

His heart kicked. "Pills? What kind of pills?"

"White," she whispered, her eyes trying to drift shut.

He lifted her to a sitting position. "How many?"

"Don't," she whimpered.

"Zara." He shook her slightly. "How many pills?"

"Six."

"Where's the bottle?" He followed her dull gaze to the floor. A quick search of the rubble produced a small prescription vial. "Is this it? These painkillers?"

She nodded.

"Come on. We're going to the hospital."

She groaned in protest as he scanned the floor for her clothes. He found the emerald silk blouse she'd worn earlier. The buttons had been torn off.

Time stopped. He was aware only of the cold rage swelling his chest, his throat, threatening to suffocate him. He drew one shaky breath, then another. Needing to be calm. For Zara.

He sat again and cupped her cheek. "I need to know. Did he rape you?"

The flash of pain in her eyes sliced him like a knife. "Answer me. Did he?"

"No," she whispered.

He hoped she was telling the truth. He already knew his brother was capable of anything.

"I was dreaming," she said thickly. "I thought he was y—" She stopped abruptly, searching his face. "Who is he?"

"Mac Byrne," he said gently. "My twin brother."

She stiffened, eyes wide with disbelief. She shook her head.

"You know it's true," he said. "You saw him. I wish to God you hadn't found out this way." If he could go back in time, he'd do things differently, be more candid with her from the start.

He wasn't accustomed to second-guessing his decisions. He wasn't accustomed to the surge of protectiveness this woman elicited from him—from a place deep within that had lain dormant so long, he'd thought that part of him was dead.

He didn't want to think about how close he'd come to apprehending Mac—his raison d'être for the last four months. He couldn't recall the precise moment when he decided to let him go in the hopes of saving Zara, but he had no doubt that given the same choice, he'd do it again.

That was something else he didn't want to think about: the telling shift in his priorities, what this woman had come to mean to him in one short weekend.

He stood. "Let's find you something to wear." He spotted her sexy little underthings on the floor. And pictured some young ER doctor plying his stethoscope over the sheer, forest green va-va-va-voom brassiere. *Breathe deeply, now.*

He turned to Emma's scattered clothes and started sifting through them. "Under the circumstances, I don't think your sister would mind sharing her things. Here we are." He held up his find: white cotton bra. Opaque. Full coverage. Ditto on the panties. A prim pink cotton blouse and khaki slacks completed the ensemble. Plus white Keds to replace Zara's high-heeled sling-backs.

She was still sitting, but appeared ready to topple.

He joined her on the bed and started to ease the quilt off her.

She drew away from him. "I don't want to go to the hospital."

"This is nonnegotiable. Your stomach pretty much emptied, it's true, but don't forget you almost drowned. You're going."

When he reached for the quilt again she clutched at it. Pointed at the door.

"Don't be silly, Zara. Let me help you." He didn't bother reminding her it was a little late for modesty. Her bleak expression brought him up short. He imagined her ordeal at Mac's hands, his eyes drawn again to the buttonless blouse. He stroked her cheek and headed for the door. "I'll leave the door open a crack, so I can hear you if you call for me, okay?"

She nodded, and he saw gratitude.

He paused in the doorway and looked at her. This wasn't the Zara Sutcliffe featured in *People* magazine and *U.S. News*. This wasn't the feisty, self-assured woman he'd come to know. Not this fragile, bedraggled waif with funky hair and mascara smudges under her bloodshot eyes.

But to him, she'd lost none of her allure. Each new thing he learned about her added a layer of complexity, a fresh dimension to a woman he'd considered a caricature only three days ago.

She intrigued him.

"I'll be right outside, Zara." He waited near the door, listening to the creak of the mattress and the rustle of clothing. His knuckles rapped the door. "You okay?"

"Yeah." After a few minutes she said, "Come on in."

He found her sitting on the edge of the bed, dressed, exhausted by her exertions. He squatted in front of her to slip her feet into the canvas sneakers and tie them. He started to lift her and she said, "I can walk."

He ignored her protests and carried her out to the car. She sagged in the seat next to him as he drove to the nearest hospital.

In the emergency room he handed over the prescription vial and described Zara's near drowning, then was made to cool his heels in the waiting room while a doctor checked her thoroughly. When they finally let him back to see her, she was asleep. At least he thought she was. As if she sensed his presence, her eyelids fluttered open and she reached out for him.

His heart flipped over. He squeezed her hand and brought it to his lips without thinking.

The doctor was a middle-aged African-American woman. Her name tag read Gloria Prince, M.D. "I'd like to admit her for a day or two. Just as a precaution. But she refuses."

Zara said, "I don't want to be here, Logan. Take me home."

Home.

A squalid, roach-infested warehouse.

"Zara—" he began.

"Please." She grasped his hand with both of hers, her dark eyes raised imploringly. "I hate hospitals. I can't rest here. Please, Logan."

He turned to the doctor. "Will she be all right if she doesn't stay?"

Dr. Prince scowled. "She seems to be out of danger, but it's routine to hold a patient for observation in cases like this. But I can't force her. Does she have someone to stay with her?"

"That'd be me," he said. "Don't worry, I'll keep a close eye on her."

Dr. Prince sighed and addressed Zara. "Don't exert yourself. You've got a good man here who's willing to wait on you. You just sit back and let him do that, you understand?"

Zara nodded obediently.

Chapter Seven

The ambrosial scent of clean sheets chased the lingering vestiges of sleep. Eyes closed, face snuggled in a pillow, Zara inhaled the mingled perfumes of Tide and Sta-Puf and knew it had all been some horrible dream. Mac Byrne. The pills. The pool.

She took a deep breath and stretched, a long, languid, feline arch. Finally she allowed her eyes to creak open.

Late morning sunlight filtered through a gauzy ivory curtain swelling with a gentle breeze. She struggled to recall that window, those curtains, this feminine bedroom. She looked down at the pastel floral sheets and matching comforter. Nothing looked familiar.

"Good morning." Logan's large form blocked the light and the breeze as he squatted next to the narrow twin bed. He touched her shoulder. "How do you feel?"

She rubbed her face and croaked, "Peachy."

"I made you some tea." He nodded toward the night table, where steam curled from an oversize stoneware mug.

"Tea?" She grimaced.

"Tea's supposed to be good for you when you're under the weather."

"I'll pass." She struggled to sit up, only then noticing that she still wore Emma's pink cotton blouse and khaki pants. "I was hoping it had all been a nightmare. Where are we?"

"Lou's house in Amityville."

"Amityville?"

"South shore of Long Island. Just over the border into Suffolk County."

He stroked her hair off her forehead, threading his fingers through the strands and over her scalp. Her eyes drifted shut. It felt like heaven.

He said, "I didn't have the heart to take you back to the warehouse. Not in the shape you were in."

She looked up at him. "Is this place safe?"

"Safe enough for the moment. Don't worry." He stood up. "You were pretty out of it when we got here last night—this morning really, about 2:00 a.m. Slept all the way from the hospital. You just kind of fell into bed as you were."

She plucked her wrinkled shirt. "Trust Emma to own clothes you can sleep in."

"Lou offered to undress you, but I said—"

"*Lou* offered? Well, wasn't that generous of him!" How many men were going to see her naked before she got her life back!

A female voice from the doorway said, "Logan, you jerk."

Zara turned to see an attractive woman, mid-thirties. Long, kinky blond hair like a cloud, pulled up at the sides and secured with a barrette.

"What?" he said defensively.

"'Lou wanted to undress you,'" the blonde mimicked. "You ever bother to tell her Lou's short for Louise?"

Logan had that put-upon male look that said, *Outnumbered!*

She strolled into the room and held out her hand. "Louise Noonan. I know who you are. And yes, you can call me Lou."

Lou had a solid handshake. She subscribed to the Emma Sutcliffe School of Fashion, with her washable navy pantsuit and sensible shoes.

Zara said, "Thanks for sharing your home."

"No problem. Logan knows I can never say no to him."

Zara watched the two of them exchange a teasing grin, steeped in shared history. Was Lou the lucky Ms. Ribbed for Her Pleasure?

She recalled the dream she'd had at Emma's, before Mac Byrne had awakened her. Logan touching her, wanting her, leaving her on the searing brink of fulfillment. She felt like a fool.

He turned to Lou. "You going?"

She nodded and laid her hand on his shoulder. "Watch your back. Don't forget. He knows you better than you know him."

He tugged a billowing strand of blond hair, an intimate gesture of long standing, Zara suspected. "Don't worry about me. Watch your own damn back."

Zara looked away, feeling like an interloper. She heard the sound of a quick kiss and didn't know whether it was on the lips or cheek. She hated herself for wondering.

Lou said, "Get some breakfast into her, Logan." She paused on her way out the door to wag a finger at Zara. "Make him cook for you. He knows his way around my kitchen."

Zara nodded and tried to smile.

When they were alone he said, "Hungry?"

"Starved."

"It's no wonder, considering you, uh…"

"You can say it." *Lost my supper? Tossed my cookies?*

"Barfed your guts up." He helped her to stand. She swayed a bit, and he steadied her. "Easy now."

"Just point me toward the bathroom."

He did more than that, he located a new toothbrush, earning her undying gratitude. She emerged a few minutes later, with her hair damp-combed and her face scrubbed free of her smeared makeup.

"My God," he said, "you look so much like Emma."

"Right down to the fetching ensemble."

"What have you got against practical clothes?"

"Life's too short for practicality. I smell coffee." She followed him to the kitchen.

"Sit," he ordered, pointing to the vinyl-cushioned dinette booth.

"Are you autocratic about *everything?* Even breakfast?" She sat, too drained to even consider defying him.

"Especially breakfast. Most important meal of the day and all that." He unerringly located an electric waffle iron in the cabinet under the microwave.

"Lou was right," she said coolly. "You certainly do know your way around her kitchen."

He opened the fridge. "Bacon? Sausage?"

"I don't know if I can stomach that much grease right now. Give me some coffee or I'll hurt you."

He grinned. "Black, right?"

"Right." He was wearing a white polo shirt. Not the gray one he had on yesterday. Which meant he probably kept clothes here.

Where had he slept last night? Not in that dinky little guest bed with her, she knew.

Stop it! she commanded herself.

He set the coffee in front of her and pulled a mixing bowl out of a cabinet. He moved to the work island where he could face her while he made the waffles.

She said, "Is my sister all right?"

She saw chagrin as he looked up from his work. "That was a mistake. Not telling you earlier."

Oh, God. *"Is she?"*

"Yes. She's fine. Safe. I told you she hooked up with Gage Foster. He took Emma home with him to Arkansas. She's safely tucked away with him somewhere in the Ozarks, waiting for me to call with word about your mother." As he talked he collected utensils and ingredients. "Which I haven't done yet. What would be the point? I don't have anything concrete to tell her."

She closed her eyes on a sigh of relief. "You have their phone number, then?"

He nodded. "We'll call after breakfast."

"What did you hope to accomplish by keeping me in the dark, Logan? By keeping me from talking to her?'' She raised her palm. ''And don't tell me it was for my protection.''

''It served my purpose.''

''Which was to keep me docile, manageable.''

''Yes.'' He broke eggs into a bowl. ''If I'd thought you were going to bolt like that...''

''Can you blame me? What would you have done?''

He measured and mixed in silence. ''You know what they say about hindsight.''

Were her ears deceiving her? ''Are you saying you made a mistake?''

He kept his eyes on the batter he was thrashing. ''I'm saying maybe I could've been more up-front, okay? Maybe if I had, it would've kept you from pulling an asinine stunt like running off to your sister's without even considering that the man who wants you dead might be watching the place.'' He glared at her.

As apologies went, it was less than impressive— yet at the same time, more than she'd hoped for. Too, she couldn't deny her foolhardiness. They were both to blame for what happened.

''You saved my life,'' she said quietly. ''Thank you.''

Something flitted over his features for a split second before he directed his gaze to the bowl. Something that told her he was more affected by her near demise than he wanted to let on.

She said, ''How did you know I'd gone to Emma's?''

''That was a no-brainer. You were determined to

talk to her." He flipped open the waffle iron and poured a sizzling cup of batter in it.

"Was Mac still there when you arrived?"

His face hardened. "Yeah. He was there."

"And he got away…?"

"I had no choice, Zara."

And then she understood. He'd let him go so he could save her. The object of his single-minded pursuit had been right there, within reach, and he'd let him get away.

For her.

She opened her mouth, and closed it. She didn't know what to say.

He offered, "He'll slip up. And when he does, I'll be there."

"What did Lou mean? When she said he knows you better than you know him?"

His jaw worked. "I must be pretty predictable, as far as my brother is concerned. Whereas Mac, well, he's more of a wild card. Let me put it that way."

"Wild card? I already figured out he's nothing like you." And she thought she and *her* twin were different!

"He's brain damaged, Zara. It happened when he was eighteen."

She was stunned, until she remembered the scar under Mac's hairline. "What happened?"

He eased up the top of the steaming waffle iron to take a peek. It was still sticking. "Mac and I…we weren't exactly the Hardy Boys growing up. We got in our share of trouble."

"*You?* What kind of trouble?"

He shrugged. "Some vandalism. Petty theft. Boosted a few cars."

"You stole *cars?*"

"Just for joyriding. Not to sell."

"Oh," she said dryly. "That's okay, then."

"There was nothing okay about it. I'm not making excuses, Zara. I did some things and took my licks. And I straightened myself out."

"And Mac?"

"There wasn't much of a gang life in Smithville, our small town, but what there was, he found. I knew those guys were bad news, and I gave them a wide berth myself. But Mac...he was into it, the whole tough-guy mystique. He wanted to be *baaad.*"

He got his wish, she thought.

He continued, "Only, in his zeal he made what one might call a tactical error."

"Which was...?"

"Seduced the gang leader's girlfriend." He lifted the crisp brown waffle out of the iron and deposited it on a plate. He circled the work island and placed it in front of her. "Syrup or powdered sugar?"

"So what happened?"

"Mac's new pals jumped him in a parking lot. Beat him to within an inch of his life, put him in a coma. He spent weeks in the hospital. Was never the same after."

His pain was still close to the surface. She could see it, in the flat expression, the too composed features.

She said, "Your parents must've been devastated."

He fetched the syrup and poured a second waffle.

"They've never gotten over it. They're very... protective of him."

"Even now? I don't understand."

"I think they're in touch with Mac. I think they could lead me to him, if they wanted to. In fact, I'm sure of it." He gazed out the window. "They despise me for what I'm doing."

She saw it then. Logan had been forced to make choices no one should have to—no brother, no son. He'd been placed in an impossible position, having to align himself against not only his malevolent brother but his parents, as well. She was deeply moved by his willingness to share this part of himself with her. She began to comprehend his aloofness, his all-consuming dedication to this mission.

She said, "What will you do when you catch up with him?"

"Have him committed. He belongs in a mental facility."

"You still love him, don't you? After everything."

He braced his arms on the countertop. "He's my brother, Zara. I should have done more. I should have kept him out of that gang."

"Sounds like Mac had a mind of his own."

"He did, and back then I told myself it was none of my business what kind of mess he got himself into. But if I'd stuck closer by him, that beating never would've happened. He'd be...he'd be normal today."

"You can't blame yourself. He made his own choices." And here was Logan, the good brother, picking up the pieces.

He didn't respond to that, just nodded at her plate and said, "Don't let it get cold."

"I'll wait for you." Her hunger had suddenly abated. "When you said you didn't think Mac would want to hurt my mother, what did you mean?"

He removed his waffle from the iron and carried his plate to the table. At last, something resembling a smile. "You've seen Candy's old movies. The skimpy outfits. The suggestive dialogue. The whole vampy, campy scream-queen thing. Eat." He dug in to his own meal.

"What do those old films have to do with this?"

"He was smitten. Well, me, too, when I was twelve and we'd watch those cheap horror flicks on TV. She sure was something."

Zara smirked. "Hey, that's my mother you're talking about!" She poured syrup on the waffle and tried a bite. It was delicious.

He said, "I think you're on the mend."

She looked at him quizzically, mouth full.

"You're doing that thing with your shoulders." He smiled at her look of chagrin. "Don't be embarrassed. I like it. It's sexy."

Averting her eyes, she squeaked the waffle down her gullet and chased it with a gulp of coffee.

"Anyway," he continued, "I got over my adolescent crush on Candy Carmelle about the time I discovered real girls. My brother, though...he was never a hundred percent grounded in reality. I think watching those movies, over and over, influenced his concept of female perfection."

"Good God."

"No matter what he may threaten, I don't think he

could bring himself to do in the object of his adora-
tion. I've seen some recent photos of Candy. Far as
I can judge, she doesn't look much different from
when she shrieked her way through those *Atomic
Bride* pictures.''

"Good genes and a better plastic surgeon," she
said. "I hope you're right."

"Mac's weirdness escalated after the beating—
what my folks so benignly refer to as his 'accident.'
He became firmly entrenched in a fantasy world—
movies, role-playing games like Dungeons & Drag-
ons, and later, computer games.''

"And your parents didn't discourage it?"

"They indulged him. A function of their own
guilty consciences, no doubt. His behavior became
more bizarre, more violent. At the same time he saw
me working hard to turn my life around. I got in with
a better crowd, improved my grades, went to college.
Eventually I joined the Bureau."

"What was Mac's reaction?"

"I think he was jealous. And that resentment
helped set him on the opposite path. He started out
as a legitimate art dealer. Educated himself, slimed
his way into the right circles. Brain damaged or not,
he was always smart, resourceful. I actually held out
hope he was a legitimate businessman, that he'd left
the rough stuff behind.''

"When did you realize he hadn't?"

Logan pushed away his empty plate. "I suspected
for some time. It just didn't scan—that he could support his lavish life-style on the amount of business he
was doing out of that little office of his. He was pretty
good at covering his tracks, but at the Bureau I had

access to state-of-the-art surveillance and information-gathering techniques. When I realized he'd diversified into stolen art and collectibles, I tried to intercede, get him to straighten out. I was determined not to make the same mistake twice. Waiting and watching until it was too late.''

"I take it he was unreceptive to your brotherly concern.''

"Understatement of the year. So I backed off. Figured, let him dig his own grave. It was only a matter of time before one of his scams would backfire and he'd be put away for a while. But as I kept tabs on him, I realized the stakes were getting higher. He'd gotten hooked up with some real nasty characters, the kind who'd think nothing of killing you if they thought you were trying to put something over on them.''

"And let me guess. Mac tries to put something over on everyone.''

"You got that right. As far as I could see, he'd pulled out all the stops. Extortion, assault, you name it. I knew then that he had to be stopped, before he did the unthinkable.''

The unthinkable. "Tell me what he did to Emma.''

"He pushed her in front of a subway train.''

Zara's hand went to her mouth, as if to contain her anguished cry.

He said, "It happened when she was on her way to meet him. He followed her onto the subway platform, snatched her bag—obviously thinking it contained the ray gun—and pushed her.''

"And—and Gage saved her, you said?''

"He'd followed her, too, thinking she was you, infuriated because you'd stood him up for your meeting. Turned out she was hiding the gun inside her raincoat.''

"But Mac got it eventually. By kidnapping Candy and holding her for ransom."

Logan slid onto a corner of the dinette bench, draping one long arm over the back. "That was the deal, Candy in exchange for the ray gun. When Gage went to meet with him, Mac got the gun."

"But didn't release Mom," she surmised.

"Right."

"Because she can identify him. But I can identify him, too, and that's why he's trying to kill me. How can you be so sure his adolescent crush on my mother will keep him from…from hurting her?"

He laid his hand on her arm. "I can't be sure, Zara. When you're dealing with someone like Mac, there are no guarantees. I'm going by my gut here—and something Mac said to Emma. He hinted that he had plans for Candy that would put her on easy street. Don't ask me what that's about."

"I'm surprised the FBI is letting you work on this case. I'd think they'd be concerned about your connection to Mac, a conflict of interest."

"I'm not with the Bureau anymore."

"What!"

"I quit a couple of years ago."

She sat straight, panic surging anew. He dropped his hand. "Are you telling me this is a one-man operation? That you don't have the FBI behind you?"

"I have contacts in all the agencies, resources to draw on. It's what I do."

"What does that mean, it's what you do?"

"I solve problems, Zara. For individuals. For companies."

She shook her head, uncomprehending.

"Corporate espionage. Celebrity stalkers. Kidnappings. Blackmail." He spread his hands. "Problems. Some things can be handled more efficiently by circumventing the official channels. There are times when the police and the D.A.'s office, even the Bureau, can compromise a delicate situation. A case of too many cooks. None of whom care enough to see the thing done right."

"What are you saying? That you work outside the law? That you're some kind of—of hired gun?"

"Not outside the law...on the fringes maybe. I have my own code of ethics and I'm comfortable with it."

"Would the authorities be comfortable if they knew what you do?"

He shrugged. "I'm careful. And discreet. It's been my bread and butter for the past twenty-two months, since I cut myself loose from the Bureau."

"What made you quit?"

He sighed. "That's a long story."

She put down her fork, leaving half her waffle. "I have all day."

"You read the papers. You know some of it already."

"What, like what happened at Waco?"

"Waco, Ruby Ridge. As tragic as incidents like that are, the real tragedy is that they're avoidable. A matter of too much stiff-necked policy-making and too little plain old horse sense. The Bureau's dragged down by this swollen, inflexible bureaucracy. The average agent in the field is swamped by paperwork and dead-end cases.''

"So you decided to quit."

He stood abruptly and started clearing their dishes. "I figured I could do more good on my own. No partners dropping the ball. No double-crossing supervisors. Just me."

He had his back to her as he loaded the dishwasher. She wondered what he wasn't telling her. The first time she'd looked into his eyes, days ago, she'd known he was a man with a wealth of stories.

Trust no one, he'd said. She was beginning to piece it all together.

"But it isn't just you, is it?" she asked his back as he wiped out the waffle iron. "You're working with Lou. Tell me she isn't on her way to my office right now, or my apartment, or somewhere else Mac might make an appearance."

"Lou's different. I'd trust her with my life. I *have* trusted her with my life, on more than one occasion."

Don't do it! "How long have you two been... involved?"

"Two years."

She was glad he couldn't see her face.

Abruptly he went still. He looked over his shoulder. "Do you mean *involved* involved?"

She could only nod.

And fight the urge to slap that smug grin off his face.

"Does that bother you?" he asked.

"Of course not." Her voice had risen an octave or two.

He turned around and leaned back against the

counter, fingers curled over the edge. His smile softened and she felt like sliding under the table, ashamed of the discomfort she was helpless to conceal.

"Lou and I go back a long way," he said.

"You don't have to explain anything to me."

"She's from my old hometown—one of that 'better crowd' I told you about? Lou believed in me. She helped me see that my talents didn't stop at hot-wiring cars."

Zara didn't want to think what talents Lou had helped him hone. "Why are you telling me this?"

"I told you damn near everything else. Why not this?"

She had no answer.

He said, "Lou and I became lovers our sophomore year at Brockport."

You asked for it, she chided herself. Then...

"Wait a minute. I thought you said you've only been together two years."

"We've been *working* together two years, since I set up shop. That fling in college lasted five hellish weeks. We couldn't get along—I think it's because we're so much alike. We nearly killed each other until we called it quits and agreed to be friends again."

"Was Lou with the FBI, too?"

"No. She was a detective with the NYPD, married to another cop, Adam Noonan. Good man. Adam got killed during a drug shoot-out seven years ago, and that's when Lou quit the force to become a P.I. She wanted to spend more time with her daughter."

"Lou has a daughter?"

"Holly. Eleven years old. She left for school before you woke up."

He pushed off the counter and came toward her, a gentle smile in place. "What made you think Lou and I were an item?"

"Well...I noticed you're wearing a fresh change of clothes...."

"I keep extra stuff in the trunk of my car."

"And, um, I guess I wondered where you slept last night."

"On the sofa in the living room."

"I'm making an ass of myself, aren't I?"

"Yeah, but don't stop on my account." He placed his palms on the table and leaned on it, smiling down at her. "It's quite a novelty, watching polished, poised Zara Sutcliffe make an ass of herself. And, I might add, flattering as hell being the cause of it."

"Why, you arrogant fool!"

He laughed then, a joyful, spontaneous laugh that lit his golden eyes and suffused his face with color, swelling a vein on his smooth forehead. Had she ever seen him laugh?

Not like this, she decided. Not with this pure, unreserved delight. He was beautiful to her then, in a starkly male way, and she couldn't take her eyes off him.

He ended on a rumbling chuckle, grinning at her sheepishly from beneath thick black eyebrows.

"You're really vile," she said, ignoring the renewed bout of mirth her words triggered. "You know everything about me and I know practically nothing about you."

"I'd say you've gotten pretty well caught up." He sobered. "I don't think I've ever told anyone so much about myself."

She detected a hint of regret. Regret that he'd spent so much of his life emotionally isolated from others, or that she'd managed to wheedle information he'd just as soon keep private? Perhaps she was better off not knowing.

She said, "Let's call Emma."

He retrieved Gage's phone number and called from the kitchen wall phone. "Gage. Logan Byrne. I have—"

Zara watched his face tighten and felt her gut respond. He glanced at her for the briefest moment.

"When?" he asked. "Did you check the airlines?" After a moment, he said, "No. You stay there. She might call." He gave Gage the phone number at Lou's and his cell phone number and hung up.

Zara found herself on her feet. "Don't sugarcoat it, Logan."

"She's gone."

"*Gone?*"

"Emma's worried about your mother—and you. She slipped away from Gage and took off for New York. What is it with you women?" he barked. "Why can't you just stay put?"

And trust the men in our lives to take care of us? Trust didn't come easily. The men in their lives had a less-than-sterling track record—starting with John Sutcliffe. "Did her plane get in yet?"

He nodded grimly. "Too late to intercept her at the airport."

"Your specialty." She tried to anticipate Emma's moves. "She doesn't know where you've been keeping me. She's going to check out my apartment, my office…"

He was already dialing the phone. "Mac's out there, just itching to finish what he started."

She slumped onto the bench and dropped her face into her hands, listening to him alert Lou. That's when she realized his associate had associates herself, surveilling various locations.

She felt Logan's hand on her shoulder. "I'll find her, Zara."

He didn't need to add, *Unless it's already too late.*

Chapter Eight

"Ronald." Emma yanked off the floppy green-and-yellow sun hat and the dark glasses. "Am I glad to see you."

"You!"

"Now, hold on—"

"I'm not talking to you!"

Indignation colored Ronald Harrington's pale face and throat and heightened his Boston accent. He stood in his apartment doorway in gym shorts and a wide leather weight lifter's belt. His bald cranium glistened, as did the tawny fur on his muscular chest and back. Apparently that which failed to take root on his head sprouted with vigorous abandon elsewhere. The designer tortoiseshell eyeglasses slid down his nose and he pushed them back up. To Emma he looked like a woolly, bespectacled Mr. Clean.

She glanced down the hallway. "Can I come in?"

His mouth dropped open. "Not likely! After that stunt with my Porsche? It needed thirty-four hundred dollars in repairs after your little jaunt. It's still in the shop. I'm very angry with you, Zara."

Down the hall the elevator doors started to open.

Emma bullied past Ronald and slammed the door shut. His apartment was identical in layout to Zara's next door, but there the similarity ended. His entire living room was filled with Nautilus machines and free weights. The walls were floor-to-ceiling mirrors.

Ronald Harrington was a partner in a prestigious Wall Street investment firm and looked the part—above the tree-stump neck. From the chin down, he was solid, pumped-up muscle, which strained the seams of his usual designer suits.

"Listen, I'm sorry about your car." Pretending to be Zara, she'd sweet-talked the keys from him to follow Gage when he went to ransom her mother.

"As well you should be. I make an effort to be neighborly and look how I'm rewarded."

She was well aware what reward he'd anticipated for his "neighborliness" but was too much of a lady to bring it up. "I need to tell you something," she said. "I'm not Zara. I'm Zara's twin sister, Emma."

He stared at her, expressionless. "Get. Out." He reached for the doorknob, and she grabbed his thick wrist.

"No! Please, Ronald. I'm being followed." She hoped it was a lie.

"I'm no longer amused, Zara. My amusement ended thirty-four hundred dollars ago."

"Oh, stop with the thirty-four hundred! You're insured."

"That's not the point."

"Ronald. Think about it. If I were Zara, how could I manage to grow my hair so quickly?"

"Wig."

She stalked up to him, tugging on her long hair. "Is this a wig? Feel."

He rolled his eyes.

"Feel it!"

Tentatively he lifted a strand and rubbed it between his fingertips. He pulled on it, gently at first, then not so gently.

"Ow! See?"

He inspected her scalp with simian concentration. "How did you do that?"

"I'm not Zara!" She jerked away from his probing fingers. "Didn't she ever mention a twin sister?"

"Never."

Emma wasn't surprised. She didn't talk much about Zara, either. She and her sister had led separate lives so long, it was easy to forget she'd been born a twin. At least that was how it had seemed before Zara asked her to impersonate her to keep the meeting with Mac Byrne.

If the last couple of weeks had taught Emma anything, it was the importance of family. She only had one sister, and she loved her, no matter how much distance—emotional as well as geographical—they might have put between themselves over the years.

Whose fault was it? Their father's certainly, at least in part. He'd made no secret that Emma was his favorite. She'd watched her sister try so hard to please him, but Zara could never do enough. His attitude had crippled the girls' relationship and brought out a rebellious streak in Zara.

Emma regretted letting her father's neuroses dictate her adult relationship with her sister—or lack of it. It often took a crisis to open one's eyes to what was important. At this point she wanted nothing more than to see her mother safely rescued…and to tell Zara she loved her.

Ronald eyed her warily as he wiped his face and dome with a towel. "You really are Zara's twin sister, aren't you."

"I really am. I need to know if you've seen her the last few days. Has she been back to her apartment?"

"Not that I've noticed."

It was the answer she'd expected. Logan had said he'd keep her somewhere safe. She wished Mac's taciturn brother had been a bit more specific.

"I've been checking my answering machine from Arkansas," Emma said, more to herself than Ronald.

"From *where?*"

"Zara left a message—I don't know when. Sounded rattled. Said she was coming over."

While she was supposed to be under Logan's protection, holed up in some safe house! Something had gone wrong. Hearing that message had been the final straw. She'd spent days anxiously awaiting word that her mother had been rescued. But Logan hadn't called, and she didn't know where to reach him.

Emma's nerves had been stretched thin when she dialed her home phone number in Queens last night and heard Zara's message. She'd insisted on flying to New York, but Gage had been adamant that she stay there in Arkansas, where she was safe. While God knew what was happening to her mother and her sister.

She and Gage had argued. Zara could take care of herself, he'd insisted, but she knew he was talking about the Zara Sutcliffe profiled on TV and in the newsmagazines. He'd never met the woman who was vying to be his agent. He didn't know, as Emma did, that behind the brash, self-confident exterior she was as insecure as Emma. Perhaps more so.

That morning, while Gage was out running a few errands, she'd taken off for the airport and grabbed the first flight to New York. Once in Queens, she'd swung by her house and found it in the same ransacked condition she'd left it—with the addition of a pile of Zara's clothes in her bedroom, looking as if they'd been torn off her.

Knowing Mac could be anywhere, she'd grabbed the hat and sunglasses as an impromptu disguise and taken a cab here to Zara's apartment building on East Eighty-sixth. Next step: her sister's office on Sixtieth and Madison. Not that she expected any sign of Zara there, either. But she had to do *something*.

She jammed the hat back on her head and slid the sunglasses on. Ronald said, "It's the hideous hat that convinced me you're not Zara. She wouldn't be caught dead in a monstrosity like that."

"Gee, thanks." So much for her bold and daring departure from natural straw. She'd never be the fashion plate her sister was. "Listen, if you do run into her..." No. He had no way to get in touch with Emma. She didn't even know where she'd be staying. "Forget it. I'll call you. Tomorrow."

She eased open the door and checked the hall. Clear. She bid Mr. Clean adieu, hurried down the hall and pushed the Down button.

Once out on the street, she headed toward the subway but wondered how much it would cost to take a taxi to Zara's office twenty-six blocks south. She struggled to summon her usual frugality, even as her mind insisted on replaying the horrific result of her last foray into the New York City subway system. Mac Byrne, dressed as a vagrant, had snatched her shoulder bag and shoved her off the platform into the path of a train. If Gage hadn't jumped onto the tracks to save her...

A block from Zara's building, her steps slowed. No, dammit. She couldn't go back into a subway tunnel. Raising her hand to hail a taxi, she stepped off the curb and scanned the oncoming traffic. A yellow cab peeled away from the phalanx of vehicles and cut across a lane. She dashed toward it, opened the back door and slid inside.

Mac Byrne scooted in right behind her and pulled the door closed. Her mouth locked open on what would have been a scream if the tip of a gun barrel hadn't been poking her ribs through the pocket of his cream linen sport jacket.

"That's what I like about you, Emma. You're the sensible one." He flipped the hat off her, onto the floor of the cab. "Except for this silly thing. It looks better in your hall closet."

Which had to be where he'd seen it last, and why he'd recognized her.

He removed her plain, dark sunglasses and perched them on his own face. One long arm snaked around her shoulders in a loverlike embrace as the gun gouged deeper. "Eightieth and Lex, driver." He peered over the top of the shades and winked broadly. "And keep your eyes on the road!"

"SHE NEEDS MORE TIME to rest, Logan. Can't you see how pale she still is?" Lou's voice was an urgent whisper.

Logan stood huddled with her in the kitchen, their voices muffled by the noise of the dishwasher. Beyond the archway into the dining room they could hear eleven-year-old Holly, a budding novelist, pumping Zara for information about the glamorous world of publishing. They'd just polished off a meal of spaghetti and meatballs.

"Do you think I want this?" he said. "I know she's in no shape to go back to that…" He scrubbed a hand over his face, weary and wishing for the miracle of a few more options. Hotels weren't safe. And they'd been at Lou's too long as it was. "The longer we're here, the more danger you're in. Mac knows I've stayed in touch with you. Who's to say he hasn't already tracked us down here?"

"Let me worry about that. I'm telling you to stay."

"Think about Holly."

Lou held his gaze a long moment before looking away, toward the archway and her daughter's excited chatter.

"You know I'm right," he said gently, and patted her arm. "Don't worry about Zara. I'll take care of her."

She gave him a lopsided smile. "Logan Byrne playing nursemaid?"

"When I think about what almost happened… She wasn't breathing, Lou. She was…I thought she was gone. Yeah, I'll play nursemaid. No problem."

Her smile changed into one almost of wonderment, but when he said, "What?" she refused to elaborate. When he thought about it, he was glad she hadn't.

"Listen, uh, Lou...I'd like to borrow a few things to, you know, fix up the warehouse a little?"

He tried not to squirm under her impassive stare. "This is gonna be good," she finally said. "Tell me. What frivolous items has Zara done without these past few days? Toilet paper? Running water?"

"Nothing like that. Man. Sheets."

A long-suffering sigh. "Pillows?" she prompted.

"Oh. Pillows, too. Sheets and pillows."

"How're you fixed for towels?"

"Towels, we have."

"Bug spray."

"Oh. Yeah. I guess we could use some of that."

Logan didn't need his old friend's dark glower to feel as low as one of those doomed cockroaches. Zara's comfort hadn't been high on his list when he'd selected the safe house. If anything, the prospect of the spoiled Ms. Sutcliffe toughing it out under such austere conditions had amused him.

But now he could only wonder...what on earth had he been thinking?

"IF YOU WANT TO CLOSE your eyes and take a nap..." Logan suggested. He put the BMW in gear and backed out of Lou's garage. It was close to ten, and fully dark. He began negotiating the suburban roads that would take him to the highway.

"Holly's a good kid." Zara smiled. "Reminds me of myself at that age. So much ambition, so much heart."

"Did you always want to be involved in publishing?"

"I always wanted to be involved with books. They

were my escape when I was a kid. My safety valve. I would just crawl between the pages of some book about dinosaurs or a Judy Bolton mystery and let everything else roll off my back.'' She looked at him. ''What was your escape?''

''Who says I needed an escape?''

She just waited for the answer. How had she come to know him so well in just a few days?

''Coins,'' he said. ''I had a coin collection.''

''Really? I can't picture it.''

''Too nerdy?''

''No...I guess it's the patience and attention to detail that don't quite fit. I see you more as a man of action.''

''Believe me, given the right provocation, I can be patient and attentive to detail.'' He slid a suggestive grin her way, and she smirked.

She asked, ''Do you still have your coins?''

''Mac stole them when I left for college.''

After a moment she said, ''I should've guessed.''

He drove in silence awhile. They got onto the parkway and he picked up speed.

Zara turned to him. ''When are you going to tell me what you need me for?''

His pulse lurched. ''What are you talking about?''

''You didn't pick me up at the airport for my safety, Logan. At least that wasn't the only reason. You need me to do something.''

He forced his hands to unclench on the steering wheel. ''Things have changed. It doesn't matter what I had in mind before.''

''Why not?''

"Because I'm no longer willing to put you at risk."
He kept his eyes on the road.

After a few moments she said quietly, "I thought
so. I knew it had to be something like that."

He took a deep breath. "My idea was to use you
to sort of…lure him out of hiding."

"We tried that. It didn't work."

"We tried it without you being physically present.
I was hoping he'd fall for that, show up at the restaurant and wait for you."

"You underestimated him."

"It would seem I did."

"And when you had me call his machine the second time…"

"There's no point in hashing all this out, Zara. I've
changed my mind."

She half turned toward him. "And when you had
me call him again," she persisted, "it was to set up
a face-to-face meeting. You figured my actual presence would do the trick."

He felt defeated. "That was the plan."

She sat back again. "I'll do it."

His gaze snapped to her profile. She was staring
straight ahead. "Like hell."

"It's my decision, Logan. My call."

"Forget it. I told you, I've changed my mind. I
won't use you like that."

"Don't worry about it," she said caustically. "Being used is what I do best. Ask Tony."

He bristled at the comparison to her detestable ex-
husband. "This isn't the same thing."

"You're right, it's not," she said, but the words
were flat. She wouldn't look at him. "Forget I said

it, okay? Your plan makes sense. We don't seem to have too many other options.''

"You already had your face-to-face with Mac. And look how it almost ended.''

"That won't happen again. You'll be there to back me up.''

"Think about it, Zara. After last night, what are the chances of Mac walking into a trap? He'd know I'm watching. Maybe he wouldn't show. Maybe he'd arrange some sort of ambush. Anything's possible. The simple fact is, we no longer have the upper hand, if we ever did. We can no longer call the shots.''

"Because I messed things up by going over to Emma's. I jumped the gun.''

"You didn't know what I had planned. If I'd been more up-front, maybe it wouldn't have happened.''

"We should be able to figure out a way to trip him up. If he knows I'm going to be at some particular location—''

"No. That's final.''

"Why?''

Because I nearly lost you once. "Drop it, Zara.''

She was silent, and he shot her a leery glance. "And don't get any ideas! You nearly got yourself killed. Once is enough.''

"You forget. It's my mother he's holding. God knows what he's done to her. I've gotten a taste of his violence firsthand. I know what she's up against. And what about Emma? You and Lou haven't been able to track her down yet. He might have gotten to her already.''

That was Gage's fear, as well. He'd been champing at the bit down in Arkansas, calling every hour.

She said, "Logan, it's my fault Mom is going through this. This whole thing is my fault."

"That's bull and you know it."

"If I hadn't agreed to sell him the ray gun—"

"He would've gone at it from a different angle. He wasn't about to walk away from it, Zara. Not with two million bucks up for grabs."

"But if I hadn't jumped at the chance to bankroll an apartment for Mom, if I hadn't asked Emma to impersonate me—"

"Dammit, this is not your fault!"

"That isn't what you said a couple of days ago."

"I said it was your fault?"

"Not in so many words. You implied it."

"Well, I'm unimplying it. The only one responsible for any of this is my brother."

"It's true, what Dad always said about me. And Tony. In some ways I guess they knew me better than I knew myself."

"What are you talking about?"

"All my life I've heard how self-centered I am. That I lack character. Moral fiber."

"This from a couple of world-class jerks. You said yourself your dad was a control freak. And Tony...talk about self-centered. Did it ever occur to you these guys just didn't know what to do with an independent woman?"

"What are you saying, that they felt threatened by me?"

"That's exactly what I'm saying."

He let that steep awhile.

"You're willing to risk your neck to help rescue your mother," he said, "even though you're frightened, and with good reason. You feel accountable and you want to make it right. That doesn't sound like someone who's short on moral fiber.''

She was quiet so long, he glanced over at her. She was smiling. "You're really sweet, you know that?'' she said. "So…adamant. Defending my character.''

Eyes on the traffic once more, he murmured, "There's nothing wrong with your character, Zara.'' He'd been so self-righteous a few days ago, so smug in his assumptions about this woman he'd never even met. You'd think he'd have known better than to accept at face value the distorted image of Zara Sutcliffe presented by the media.

He added, "But a word of warning. Not only am *I* not threatened by independent women, I'll chain this particular independent woman to the goddamn radiator if she gets even the slightest urge to strike out on her own. Am I coming in loud and clear?''

Zara just laughed.

Chapter Nine

"How long does he usually stay away?" Emma listened to the receding sound of automobile tires on gravel. She'd just spent her first night in the basement prison with her mother. Her relief at finding Candy unharmed had quickly given way to despair at the unlikelihood of rescue.

"Hours usually," Candy answered from the middle of the floor, where she was doing stretching exercises. "Sometimes nearly the whole day. I figure he goes into the city."

"A good long drive each way." Emma couldn't be certain where this house was. She'd ridden nearly the entire distance in the trunk of Mac's car—a singularly horrifying experience. She suspected they were in Rockland or Putnam County, north of the city. "You sure he didn't hurt you at all?" She must have asked this question a dozen times since being reunited with her mother. She was well aware of Mac's propensity for violence.

"Not a scratch." Candy took a break and sat cross-legged on the floor. "I'm pretty sure he's a serious fan of mine. Smitten even."

Emma's jaw dropped. "Get out!"

"I recognize the signs. I could be wrong, but my gut tells me I'm not. And even if I am, it's in his interest to keep me in one piece. Like I told you, there's someone out there willing to pay eight million bucks for a living, breathing Candy Carmelle."

Since Emma's arrival yesterday evening, she and Candy had shared what information they had. When Emma had told her about Gage, Candy had expressed delight in finally learning the identity of Mac's "damn cowboy."

"But what about me?" Emma crossed to the ratty sofa and plopped down. "Why am I even here? I thought for sure Mac was going to kill me yesterday. He tried to once."

"Something must've happened." Candy rose and joined her daughter on the sofa. "Something that makes you more valuable alive than dead. Thank God." She squeezed Emma's hand, her eyes shiny.

"The mysterious William perhaps?"

Her mother eased her hand away. She averted her eyes, but not before Emma detected conflicting impulses battling it out behind them.

"What? Mom, what aren't you telling me?" She touched Candy's arm. "You know something about this William, don't you?"

"No. Maybe. It's just a...crazy suspicion. I must've been down here too long." She smiled weakly. "It's affecting my mind."

Emma sat up and made her mother face her. "I want all of it."

Candy took a deep breath. "It's just that I knew a William. Long ago. Only he called himself Billy then.

Billy Sharke. I overheard Mac say something to William about trying to live up to his name…''

"Sharke." It took a moment to click. "Billy Sharke! He was a director. *The Slithering,* right?"

"And a handful of other pictures, including *Return of the Atomic Bride.*"

"The movie that ray gun was used in."

"Right."

"So, what? Were you and Billy close? Did you two have a thing going?"

Candy turned pink. She was embarrassed! Emma couldn't recall her mother ever being embarrassed about anything, least of all anything having to do with sex.

"Wow. That must've been some affair," Emma said. "So why do you think it might be the same guy? Is he loaded?"

"I don't know. He could be, I suppose. He sure wasn't then."

"You mean you haven't kept in touch over the years?"

Candy's bleak expression brought Emma up short. "Mom? What is it?"

"There are things I never told you. About John."

"Dad? What about him?"

"Honey, he wasn't the man you thought he was. You have no idea what he was capable of."

"Oh, I have a pretty good idea. You only knew him for a couple of years, after all, Mom. We were raised by him. By the time he died…I hate to say this…I don't think I loved him anymore. It was that bad."

"It was worse, only you never knew. There were things that were kept from you."

Emma was shocked by the depth of bitterness behind her mother's words. "Like what?"

"John used his wealth and position in society—his power—to control everything and everyone around him. He had no scruples. He was a…a megalomaniac."

Emma had never applied that particular term to her father, but she couldn't deny the description fit. "I know he cheated you out of custody of me and Zara. He kept you from even seeing us. What else did he do?"

"Seizing custody was child's play for him. What didn't he do? He manipulated everyone, all his personal and business dealings. Methodically bankrupted anyone who defied him, even people he'd known all his life. It was a power game for him. If I'd only known before I married him… He could be so charming when he wanted something. And thirty years ago, he wanted me."

"How does Billy Sharke fit into this?"

"John was fanatically jealous of Billy. He thought I was still in love with him." Candy stared off toward the utility room as she spoke.

"Were you?" Emma asked gently.

"Yes. But I made my choice. Billy was a director of grade B horror flicks, struggling to pay his rent just like everyone else. And there was John Sutcliffe, with his mansion and money and everybody kowtowing to him. It was all I'd ever dreamed of since I was a little girl living in a crowded fifth-floor walk-up in Little

Italy. Security. Respectability. I figured this was my one and only shot."

"And you took it. Who could blame you?"

"I blamed myself after what he did to Billy." Tears spilled down her cheeks. "John ruined him. He—he had him blacklisted in Hollywood. He bought off producers, engineered vicious rumors about drug use and...and other things too horrible to mention. And he maimed him," she whispered.

Emma swallowed hard, knowing she didn't want to hear any more, but knowing her mother needed to talk about this.

Candy dried her eyes and cleared her throat. "John had some hired thugs break Billy's legs. They shattered them with baseball bats. And he made me watch."

"Oh, my God..."

"He said if either one of us ever tried to contact the other, he'd kill us both. There was never a question he could and would do it. Efficiently. Anonymously."

Emma felt out of breath. She realized she was squeezing Candy's hand hard. Her mother seemed not to notice. She stared into space as if transported to another place, another time.

"So I never tried to find him," she whispered. "Even after the divorce. John never stopped watching me, keeping tabs on me. I knew if I looked for Billy, he'd find out and..."

"I can't—I can't believe Dad would do something like that," Emma said. But it was a lie. A part of her knew her father had indeed been capable of such acts.

"I've thought about it, since John's death. I've

thought about looking for Billy. But what would I tell him?'' She broke down, sobbing into her hands. ''What could I say that would make up for...''

Emma pulled her into her arms and held her tight. Could this mysterious William be Billy Sharke? It seemed too bizarre to be true, and yet she could say that about almost everything that had happened the past couple of weeks.

Her mother struggled to compose herself. She drew away and straightened her back, and for the first time Emma saw all sixty-one years in her tear-streaked face.

Candy looked directly into her daughter's eyes and said, ''There's more.''

''YOU KNOW, YOU DON'T HAVE to do everything for me, Logan. I feel fine.''

Zara sat cross-legged in the middle of the bed, an incongruously plush oasis set amid the squalid desert of the warehouse. When they'd arrived last night, Logan had double-bagged the nasty mattress with two quilted covers, then made up the bed with Lou's delicate rose-patterned sheets, her mother-in-law's handmade quilt and four fluffy pillows.

That was for Zara, of course. He'd spent the night in his sleeping bag on the floor. It was after 11:00 p.m., and she'd just endured a second day of ex-Special Agent Logan Byrne's militant brand of pampering. She hadn't been allowed to lift a finger.

He looked up from her luggage, where he was searching for her nightclothes. ''Lou wouldn't let us leave till I promised to take good care of you. Don't want to get her mad at me. You should've been in bed an hour ago.''

"But I'm not tired. I haven't *done* anything to-day!''

The cell phone rang.

She said, "Let's hope that's Lou.'' She didn't need to add, *With news about Emma.*

He crossed to the desk and flipped open the phone. "Yeah.''

His entire body seemed to snap to attention. Zara knew instantly it wasn't Lou.

"Meet with me, Mac. Just you and me. You name the place. The time.''

She found herself on her feet, heart punching her rib cage.

Phone clutched to his ear, Logan turned tight circles like a caged lion, his face etched in frustration. "Don't do this, man. It's just you and me. That's all. Name the time. Name the place, Mac. I'll be there. Unarmed. I want to— *Dammit!*'' He slammed the phone on the desk so hard, she was surprised it didn't shatter.

"What does he want?'' Her voice wobbled.

"He wants to rub my nose in it,'' he growled. "He has Emma.''

Her despairing wail echoed in the huge empty room.

Logan started pacing. "He has my phone number. How?''

"Who have you given it to?''

He stopped dead in his tracks. "My parents.''

"Then you were right. They are in touch with Mac.''

"I'm going there. And this time they're gonna give me some answers!" He shoved the phone into its leather case.

"Now?" she said. "You're going now?"

"I'll be back as soon as I can, Zara. I have to—"

"I'm going with you."

"No. Out of the question."

"Didn't you already try to get them to talk to you? Maybe I can help."

"You're going to stay here where you're safe."

"I'm just as safe with you, Logan. I'm coming with you. I have to. My mother…and now Emma. I can't just sit here waiting, wondering…"

She didn't realize she was shaking until he put his hands on her shoulders. He drew her against him, slowly, with infinite tenderness. "Trust me, Zara. I'll do everything in my power to end this, to see your mother and your sister safe."

She'd spent a good part of the day thinking about what Logan had revealed last night in the car. He'd detained her in this warehouse not for her protection, as he'd initially claimed, but for the express purpose of using her as bait to draw his brother out of hiding. Gullible as always, she'd bought his story about this being some sort of safe house. One would think she'd have learned long ago not to take a man at his word. There was always a self-serving motive for everything.

The irony was that four days ago she would have been paralyzed with fear at the prospect of becoming actively involved in this dangerous venture. Now she found herself arguing with him, begging him to accept her assistance.

It would seem her near demise at the hands of his brother had reconfigured Logan's priorities. Still, she couldn't ignore the indignities to which he'd subjected her. He'd hustled her from the airport using falsified ID, withheld critical information and deceived her at every turn.

Worst of all, he'd allowed her to think he cared about her, at least about her personal safety, when all along he'd planned to use her in a dangerous scheme to apprehend his brother.

The familiar feeling of being used made her stomach clench. Even after the harsh lessons of the last few years, she was as naive as some starry-eyed schoolgirl. A foolish romantic corner of her soul still wanted to believe that somewhere out there was a man who could be trusted. A man who would respect her and, in turn, be worthy of her respect.

And God help her, at that moment, as she stood in the circle of lamplight with Logan, cradled against his broad chest, enveloped in the warm security of his arms, she believed him. She trusted him. Despite everything.

She knew that if anyone could rescue her family, it was this man.

But she refused to sit idly by when her involvement could make a difference. "I can't stay here alone. Please take me with you, Logan." She met his gaze, her own level and determined. "I think I can help. Let me try at least."

He scowled, but she saw she was getting through to him.

"I won't be in any danger, anyway," she added. "I'll be with you."

He smiled grimly. "A genuine guarantee of safety." He brushed her hair off her face, cherishingly. "I'm not going to talk you out of this, am I."

She shook her head, and teased, "You could always do what you threatened and chain me to the radiator."

"A tempting thought." But he was grinning now. He lowered his head until his lips met hers. It was a gossamer kiss, a mere whisper of sensation that drizzled over her body like warm honey.

He remained motionless, his mouth barely touching hers, his very stillness intensifying the satin texture of his lips, the tantalizing taste she needed more of.

She couldn't remain still; she didn't have Logan's self-discipline. Her mouth moved, lightly, experimentally. His breath snagged and his lips parted as if of their own volition. Clearly he was fighting it, this thing between them, and having no more success than she.

Zara needed this so much it frightened her. Logan had become her rock, her anchor; if she let go of him, she'd surely be swept away in the tidal wave of insanity her world had become.

Unthinkingly she increased the pressure of her mouth, nibbled his lower lip. His long, strong fingers slid over her scalp to hold her to him. His palm on her back pressed harder as he wrested control of the kiss from her, angling his head to take her mouth with pulse-pounding thoroughness.

He dragged his hand down her spine and under her black silk tunic to fondle her bottom through her stretchy white leggings. His touch was intimate, unrepentantly brazen. She gasped into his mouth and arched against him.

"What have you done to me?" he groaned, tilting her head back to nuzzle her throat. She was breathless. Raw heat pooled in her most intimate places. Her nipples peaked and pushed against the confines of her bra. She couldn't ignore the maddening tingle or the deep hum of desire between her legs. Her arms encircled his neck.

He pressed delicate, unhurried kisses to her eyes, her cheeks, the corners of her mouth, as his hands slid up her sides under her loose tunic. When he met the obstacle of her bra, he deftly unclasped it. His fingertips continued their journey, gliding up the outside edges of her breasts, tracing the tender curve of ultrasensitive flesh there.

She stopped breathing. She gripped his shoulders, half-afraid her legs would give out. He had magic hands, a conjurer's hands. They moved on to the gentle slopes of her breasts, still with the lightest of touches, butterfly strokes. Her pent-up breath escaped in a hoarse plea. "Logan!"

"You're sensitive," he murmured. She concurred with a groan of raw pleasure. He caressed her but ignored the prickly tips of her breasts, which rasped against the lace of her loosened bra as he lifted and stroked her.

She gasped softly, momentarily startled by the warm trickle of moisture that was her body's silent invitation. As if he knew, one large hand skated down her back and over her bottom. Those magic fingers slid between her legs with just enough pressure to launch her sanity into the stratosphere. Her shuddering cry bounced off the bare walls and resounded in the big room.

He captured her mouth in a lingering kiss as his hands left her body. She swayed toward him, dizzy with longing. She knew what he saw when he looked at her: a mirror image of his own sharp hunger. The flared nostrils. The parted lips. And his eyes, deceptively languorous, but with an underlying potency that rocked her.

He fingered the neckline of her tunic. "Take this off." He stepped back, into the shadows, leaving her standing alone in the ring of lamplight.

Without hesitation she raised her fingers to the row of tiny tortoiseshell buttons. He watched intently as she eased each one through its buttonhole. Finally she let the silk slide off her shoulders to puddle on the floor. With a nod he told her to shed the bra, and she did.

She stood there exposed to the waist, spotlighted by the floor lamp. In all her nearly thirty years she'd never done this, never bared herself and waited passively, submissively, while a man simply looked at her. Sex with Tony had always been a straightforward affair, the preliminaries bypassed or glossed over.

She couldn't see Logan clearly, but she felt his gaze like a hot tongue. Her breasts shuddered with each agitated breath, her nipples stiff and tender. Each second of charged silence magnified her arousal until she thought she might explode in orgasm, without him even touching her.

If there was anything more important than having this man inside her, *right now,* she didn't know what it was.

"Come here." His voice was thick.

She walked into the gloom, drawn by his golden eyes, which glowed like live coals. She stopped inches from him, her senses clamoring for his touch, for the feel of him, the taste of him, the weight of him on her, the unyielding pressure of him in her.

He touched the aching peak of her breast, shooting a spark from his fingertip straight downward. She couldn't keep quiet. Or still. He cupped her in his palms and thumbed the tips, pinching them lightly. She grasped his wrists. It was too much. Not enough. She was practically sobbing with need.

He brought her hand to her breast and brushed the palm across the sharp tip. "You are so beautiful," he whispered, his tone one of wonder. "Perfect."

His other hand slid downward and settled between her legs. When he drew it away, one finger trailed upward, wringing a sharp gasp from her.

He placed her hand on his erection, which strained the fabric of his jeans. He felt impossibly full and heavy and vital, his flesh leaping against her fingers. Holding her gaze, he slid her palm the length of his penis. It was a primal gesture, a warning, alerting her to the seriousness of his intent.

He cupped her face and kissed her. "Do you have protection?"

Her mind struggled to assimilate the practical question. The haze of passion began to burn away like fog in bright sunlight. "No."

He started steering her toward the bed. "It's okay, I do."

"I know." She winced, wishing she could retract the hasty words.

After a silent, heart-stopping moment, a deep chuckle rumbled through his chest. "That's right, I forgot about your inquisitive nature."

Embarrassment chased the last of the fog. "I—I didn't mean to snoop."

"Of course you did." He pulled her against him and kissed the top of her head. "Hope you weren't too shocked by what you turned up."

"Not shocked…curious maybe."

"I'm flattered."

"Oh, don't start that again."

"Why not? It's flattering being the object of a beautiful woman's irrepressible curiosity."

Holding her close, he backed up to the mattress and fell with her to lie sprawled on Mother Noonan's quilt. In a flash he rolled her beneath him and maneuvered himself between her legs. He ground against her, letting her feel the throbbing power of his need for her.

His earthy abruptness triggered thoughts of another time. Another bed. Another man. The last of her desire shattered, too fragile to withstand the crushing weight of her memories.

"Logan, I—"

He silenced her with a hard, demanding kiss as his hands roamed freely. She lay limp and unresponsive. Gradually he raised his head and let his eyes do the asking.

"I can't," she said. "I can't do it."

"Zara…" he groaned, squeezing his eyes shut and dropping his forehead to hers. After a moment he rolled off her and lay staring at the ceiling, his breathing ragged.

"I'm sorry." Stiffly she reached for her tunic.

He massaged his forehead. "Don't say that!"

Her back to him, she shoved her arms in the sleeves and swiftly did up the tiny buttons. When she was almost done she realized they were out of alignment. Exasperated, chagrined and frustrated beyond measure, she cursed and started unbuttoning, double time.

He sighed. "Zara." She felt his knuckle skip down the bumps of her spine. "You have no reason to be sorry. You know that. Right?"

She didn't trust her voice.

"Right?" he repeated.

She nodded.

"Things just got…out of hand. I guess it's a good thing one of us was able to exercise mind over hormones."

She sagged. It was just as well he considered her reticence the result of superior willpower.

"Say something," he implored. "I hate it when you clam up like this."

"Why do we have to talk about it?"

He swore softly. "We don't have to talk about it, dammit. I don't want to *talk* about it. I just want to know…I don't know what I want to know. Okay?"

"You're angry."

"I'm not angry!" In a milder tone he added, "I'm frustrated."

"So am I."

Behind his mirthless half laugh was an unspoken question: *Why? If you wanted it, why did you make me stop?*

She said, "I thought I could. I wanted to. It's me, not you. I have too much…baggage. That's all."

He was silent a long time. Finally she looked over her shoulder to see him lying on his back, watching her, his expression unreadable.

He asked, "You want to tell me about it?"

She swallowed hard and turned away. "No." She closed her eyes for a moment. The tears were too close to the surface, the pain too fresh, even after so long. Taking refuge in the mundane, she lifted her bra from the floor and started to rise. She'd change, wash up and get ready to leave.

His hand on her hip stopped her. "Is it my brother? You told me he didn't—"

"He didn't. This isn't about him."

At length she heard the rustle of movement, felt the mattress shift as he sat up. "Who?"

She barely heard her own watery whisper. "I've never told anyone." *Don't make me say it now.*

She felt his hands on her shoulders, trying to pull her against his chest. She resisted, stiff and unyielding. He relented and simply sat behind her, his warm breath stirring her hair.

"Tell *me*," he murmured.

The ugliness had festered inside her so long, it had become a part of her, changing her forever, setting limits—defining the woman she now was. She could never go back, never again experience the simple joy in her sexuality she'd once taken for granted.

She tried for a light tone. "I'll pass."

"Who hurt you, Zara?"

She started to rise. He stopped her with a gentle hand and turned her to face him.

She sighed. "Why can't you just drop it?"

"Because you can't. On the surface maybe, but not inside. Whatever happened to you, it's cut real deep."

She pushed her fingers through her disheveled hair. "Logan. You're a problem solver. You think if you throw enough manpower or firepower or, I don't know, *ingenuity* at any problem, it'll just go away." Feeling her throat tighten, she said, "Not all problems can be made to go away. Some you just have to learn to live with."

He stared at her. She could tell he wasn't used to being thwarted. Finally he said, "When you're ready to talk about it, I want to listen."

The last thing she intended to do was parade her shame before this of all men, this conjurer who'd managed to reignite her long-dormant libido.

"Thanks for the offer." She pulled away from him and headed toward the bathroom. "I'll be ready in five minutes."

Chapter Ten

The man who stood in the doorway was rangy and rawboned, his salt-and-pepper hair sleep-rumpled. Zara saw an unmistakable resemblance to Logan and Mac in the eyes and the strong lines of the face. A thin flannel bathrobe covered striped pajamas. He spared Zara a brief, apathetic glance, before fixing his gaze on Logan. There was nothing apathetic—or paternal—in the look he gave his son.

"It's 1:00 a.m."

"This can't wait." Logan shoved his way past his father, pulling Zara along in his wake. Clearly he didn't expect an invitation. They entered a shabby living room with slipcovered furniture and pressboard paneling.

The old man said, "I don't want your mother upset."

"If you don't want her upset, don't harbor fugitives from the law."

Loathing added ten years to his father's weathered face. "I'm ashamed to call you my son."

Shocked, Zara looked at Logan. His implacable expression never changed. The chasm between these two was deep and wide. Whatever familial intimacy they'd once shared was long gone.

"Douglas…?"

She looked up to see an older woman standing at the top of the stairs, zipping her green velour robe. Her tired eyes widened as she took in the scene below.

Douglas waved her away. "Go back to bed, Maddie."

She hesitated a moment, and started to retreat.

Zara sensed her best hope was about to slip away. She approached the bottom of the steps. "Mrs. Byrne?"

Douglas started toward her. "What the hell—"

Logan grabbed his arm. The old man jerked as if he'd been burned. Zara wondered when the father and son had last touched. She climbed two steps.

"Mrs. Byrne. I…I know this isn't easy for you. But I'm asking you, please, give us a few minutes. Let us…let me talk to you."

Mrs. Byrne clutched the collar of her robe as if armoring herself. She asked Logan, "Who is this person?"

"My name is Zara Sutcliffe. I'm in trouble and I need your help."

Mrs. Byrne said, "Your troubles are no concern of mine." She turned to go back to her room.

Zara advanced one more step. "Is your son Mac a concern of yours? He tried to kill me, Mrs. Byrne. If it weren't for Logan, he'd have succeeded."

Douglas raged, *"Get out! You lying—"*

Logan restrained him. "We're not going anywhere till we get some answers, Dad, so just settle down."

Zara never took her eyes off Logan's mother. "I know what it's like to love someone who's...difficult to love. It never gets easier. But at a certain point you have to say, I've given all I can."

The old woman raised her chin. "I'll never give up on my son. That's not the kind of family we are." With a distasteful look at Logan, she amended, "That's not the kind of parents we are."

"No one can blame you for loving Mac, or wanting to protect him," Zara said. "I love my family, too. I have a mother, a twin sister. They—" She choked on the emotion erupting within her. "He has them. Both of them. Mac kidnapped—"

"That's not true!" Madeline Byrne gripped the white-painted metal banister for support.

Zara struggled to contain her tears. "I wish to God it weren't true. We don't know where they are. We don't know where he's holding them."

Mrs. Byrne stared at Zara, through her really, shaking her head. It was a mechanical gesture, lacking conviction.

Zara forged ahead. "Did Mac ever say anything about a movie prop? A ray gun from an old horror movie?"

Madeline looked at Douglas. He stared back, sending his wife a silent message.

Zara said, "It's a long story, but someone's willing to pay two million dollars for that gun. Mac has progressed from theft to kidnapping to attempted murder over it. I just want—" She pressed a hand to her mouth, but it was no use; the fragile thread of her control had snapped. "I just want them to come home," she managed to say around gulping sobs.

Logan started toward her, but she held him off with a raised palm. With effort she composed herself and took a deep breath. "My mother's name is Candy. My sister is Emma," she told the Byrnes, urging them to envision their son's victims as actual people. "Emma and I were raised without our mother. We reestablished contact with her just five years ago. I've barely…barely had time to get to know her."

If Candy survived this horror, Zara would let her live with her as long as she wanted—no complaints. As far as she was concerned, her mother could *wallpaper* the place with her preposterous posters.

Madeline seemed to deflate, sinking onto the top step, hugging the banister. More than anything, she simply looked tired. "We don't know where he is."

Douglas quickly interjected, "We told you. We're not in touch with him. Mac hasn't been here in months."

Logan asked, "Well, one of those times that he wasn't here, he got my phone number from your message board." He peered into the kitchen. "It's still there, I see. I was hoping you'd use it yourselves."

Douglas glared at his son, his jaw working.

Logan said, "If you have information that can help us locate Mac, and you choose not to share it, you're responsible for whatever happens to Candy and Emma. It's unlikely Mac will let them live—they can identify him. He's attempted murder twice so far that I know of. I don't imagine he'll fail a third time."

Douglas's expression was stoical—except for the eyes. They gave away his internal torment. After a silent, prayer-filled minute, Madeline said quietly, "We don't know where he is. He won't tell us."

"Maddie..." Douglas warned, but his vehemence had evaporated. Like his wife, he seemed inexpressibly weary.

Logan placed his hand on his father's shoulder, and the old man flinched. "Help us end this. For your sake. For all of us. And for Mac."

Douglas's shoulders slumped. "What can we do? He doesn't tell us much. He could be—" he raised his arms "—anywhere."

"Didn't he say anything to indicate a general location? City? Suburbs? He can't be too far from the city. He seems to come and go on a regular basis."

"Nothing," Douglas said. "Not a hint."

Madeline said, "He told us he was living at his co-op in Manhattan."

"Did you believe him?"

Their silence was eloquent. Zara could only imagine Logan's pain in knowing his parents had, through their unquestioning support, abetted Mac's criminal activities.

Logan said, "You don't have a phone number for him?"

They shook their heads.

"How often has he been coming around?"

Madeline said, "About once a week."

"When was he here last?"

His father's gaze slid away. "Earlier today."

Those two words hung in the air like a foul odor. Logan's features tightened. Zara knew what he was thinking. If his folks had just cooperated with him...

Candy and Emma could be free now. Safe.

Madeline slowly pushed to her feet. "I'll make some coffee."

Zara moved aside to let her pass on the stairs. She could have told her coffee was the last thing Logan wanted. He was interested only in answers, but those, unfortunately, were in short supply.

Like a mourner, Mrs. Byrne seemed to be relying on routine activity to keep her mind occupied. Perhaps she, too, was plagued by unwelcome thoughts—guilt at her complicity, regret for the man Mac might have been. The time for self-delusion was past. She could no longer ignore her troubled son's true nature.

Logan asked, "Has Mac been staying overnight?"

Douglas said, "Sometimes."

"Dad, you stay with Mom. I'm going to check out the bedroom, see what I can turn up."

"I don't think you'll find much," Douglas said. "He's very neat, your brother."

Logan's expression gentled for the first time since he set foot in his parents' home. Despite everything, Zara sensed he was moved by their grief. "Keep Mom company. I think she needs you."

Zara followed him up the stairs. The room he led her into was small, furnished with twin beds and an eclectic mix of timeworn furniture: desk, dresser, bookcases. The walls were devoid of artwork. If the boys had once hung posters, they were history. No trace of the young Logan remained.

She asked, "Did you share this room with Mac?"

He nodded. "In a dinky house like this, separate rooms were out of the question."

"That must've caused some strain."

He smiled at the understatement. "You could say that."

She followed his lead, helping him search the room

thoroughly. They scrutinized the contents of every drawer, peered under the furniture, stripped the beds and rolled up the throw rug. Logan pulled Mac's extensive comic-book collection off the shelves and shook out each one.

"There must be hundreds there," she said.

He held up one for her to see. The cover art featured an exotic science fiction scenario: a hair-raising alien monster and a half-naked space babe. Claws and cleavage. "He was into these strange comics just like he was into the movies and all that other check-your-brains-at-the-door stuff. He could sit here in this little room and lose himself for hours in this crap."

He stuffed the comics back on the shelves. "But the worst was the computer games. Back when home PCs first became available, he pressured Mom and Dad to buy him state-of-the-art hardware, on credit, even though it strapped them." He grimaced. "They were overjoyed that he was showing intellectual initiative. They had no idea he wanted it just to play his bizarre games. He quickly got hooked on those. Still is, as far as I know."

They emptied the closet and refilled it. Nothing. No store receipt. No restaurant matchbook. No clue as to Mac's whereabouts.

"Your father's right," she said. "He's neat."

"Intentionally, no doubt. He had to know that sooner or later I'd come here, looking for clues. His calling me was practically an invitation."

Zara lifted her fingers and smoothed the lines of his face, erasing the fierce scowl etched into his forehead and around his mouth. His gaze settled on her and softened.

She could have this, at least. This closeness, this camaraderie. For as long as it lasted.

Still staring at her, he pressed her palm to his mouth and kissed it. It was a simple gesture, one might even say innocent. But there was nothing innocent about the sparks that shot down her arm and raced over her body. There would never be anything innocent in her response to this man. It was a bittersweet fact of life.

She asked, "Are we going to search the whole house?"

He sighed. "There's no point. He's obviously covered his tracks." He stared around the room, as if he could see through walls. "He's probably out there somewhere right now, laughing at me."

"Come on. Let's get out of here and let your folks get some sleep."

"There is one more thing I need to check."

Downstairs they found Douglas and Madeline in the kitchen, talking in hushed tones. They held hands across the table. Sudden tears clogged Zara's throat. Their quiet grief brought to mind, once again, the mourning process.

The analogy was uncomfortably vivid. She couldn't shake the sense of impending death. Intellectually she knew the mission she and Logan were engaged in was rife with danger, but fear for her family had nudged that unpalatable fact into the recesses of her mind.

However, here, in Logan's boyhood home, as she watched his parents cope with the horrible reality they helped to create, that gut-clenching, palm-dampening fear resurfaced, stronger than ever. She wanted to flee into the dark, into the dead middle of the night, and not look back, even as she knew she intended to see this thing through to the end, no matter what.

She found Logan staring at her, as if he could read her mind. He reached for her hand and gave it a squeeze.

Her rock.

In return, she offered a tentative smile.

He asked, "Dad, have you taken out the garbage since Mac left?"

"Yeah. It's outside."

She followed Logan as he let himself out the side door, where the porch light illuminated a beige plastic garbage can. He pushed up the sleeves of his windbreaker, lifted the can and emptied it onto the cracked asphalt driveway.

She said, "Forgive me if I sit this one out."

He grinned at her. Good heavens, the man could even look gorgeous squatting over a pile of garbage, pawing through grapefruit peels. "Wouldn't want you to mess up your manicure."

The clatter of miniblinds drew their eyes to a dim second-floor window next door. Moonlight glinted off blue hair in curlers.

Logan turned and waved jauntily. "Why, hello there, Mrs. Morgan. Glorious night, isn't it? How's that enchanting daughter of yours?"

The window slammed shut and the blinds dropped.

Zara shook her head. "You must've been one holy terror growing up."

"Nonsense. The neighbors adored me." He tossed aside coffee filters and milk cartons.

She imagined poor Mrs. Morgan fretting over the

virtue of her enchanting daughter with the twin hellions next door sniffing around.

Logan sat on his heels. He scratched his nose with his clean forearm. *"Nada."* Puffing his cheeks with frustration, he grabbed the garbage can to begin refilling it, when something inside snagged his attention. He tilted the can toward the light and peered into it, then snaked his arm deep into the foul thing.

"Ewww..." Zara shuddered with revulsion.

He retrieved a half-inch-long scrap of paper that must have adhered to the bottom of the can. Examining it closely, he called to his mother.

She appeared behind the screen door. "What is it?" Her dismayed gaze took in the trash littering her driveway.

"I don't recognize this name." He raised a fingertip, displaying the soiled price sticker. "Abernathy Books. Is that a new store in town?"

"No..." Her brow wrinkled.

"He brought you a book, remember?" Douglas said from behind her. "A cookbook."

"Yes, that's right. A Southwestern cookbook. Mac loves my chili. Oh." She clutched the collar of her robe. The significance of the find had just sunk in.

Cold triumph glittered in Logan's eyes. "Abernathy Books. Get me the county white pages."

Chapter Eleven

Abernathy Books wasn't in the Orange County white pages. The next step was to check the phone books of neighboring counties. Madeline suggested they stay over and visit the library when it opened the next morning, but Logan was already dialing Lou's number. As a P.I., she had the national directory available on computer software. He knew she wouldn't complain about being jangled awake in the middle of the night, and she didn't. He waited a couple of minutes while, yawning, she booted up her Pentium and slipped a disk into the CD-ROM.

He hung up with a smile on his face. "Hobart. Rockland County."

Rockland was the next county east, closer to New York City. They'd driven through it on their way to the Byrnes'.

In minutes they were on their way. Zara fell asleep almost immediately. He glanced at her, slumped like a rag doll in her shoulder harness. He knew she was still weak. He'd promised both Lou and that ER doctor that he'd take care of her. Perhaps he should have taken Madeline up on her offer and stayed the night.

No. It was better this way. Zara wanted an end to this as badly as he did. And they weren't going to end it by lazing around the old homestead.

Zara had been right, he thought with wonder. She'd gotten through to his folks when all his efforts had failed. Simply by reaching out to them, expressing empathy with their plight and faith in their basic humanity. It was something he couldn't have done, being too close to them and at odds for so long.

He punched buttons on his CD pad and Dave Grusin's "Mountain Dance" wafted softly from the BMW's speakers. The music was soothing and invigorating at the same time; just what he needed.

THE SHOWER in the Shangri-La Motor Hotel was a forlorn dribble, but cold enough to jazz Logan awake. He wrapped a thin, motel-quality towel around his waist and reentered the bedroom, where Zara lay curled up under the covers of one of the two double beds.

Before leaving the warehouse, he'd called Gage with the news that Mac had Emma. That had been rough. He'd heard in Gage's Southern-tinged voice the same anguish and impotent rage he'd felt himself when he saw Zara floating facedown in her sister's pool.

The comparison didn't sit well with him. Gage and Emma had a relationship. As far as he could tell, they were in love. Whatever Logan felt for Zara, it wasn't the same thing. It couldn't be. He wasn't like Gage. He'd seen too much of life's unforgiving side, endured too much betrayal. Perhaps he'd once been that kind of man, the kind who could be there for a woman

like Zara Sutcliffe. The kind who could offer her the
love she needed and deserved. The kind who could
help heal the hurts that ate away at her.

For the first time ever, he wished he were still that
kind of man.

He sat next to her and watched her sleep. The day
was overcast, and anemic light filtered through the
drapes, softening her features and making her look
heartbreakingly vulnerable. She should be back in her
fancy penthouse apartment, he thought as he whisked
a strand of hair off her cheek, or behind the cluttered
desk in her hectic office. She should never have been
touched by this horror.

She made a face in her sleep, one eyebrow arching
imperiously. He smiled and stifled a chuckle. Was she
reacting to his touch? Even unconscious, she pushed
him away. Twice now she'd rebuffed him, and he
knew it wasn't because she was uninterested or unresponsive. The truth was, he'd never known a more
passionate, responsive woman. He wished she'd tell
him the cause of her panic, though he had a pretty
good idea, and it burned a hole in his gut to think
about it.

He didn't want to wake her, but the sun was climb-
ing and he had plenty of legwork to do today. He was
itching to get started. They were in the small town of
Hobart, and he could practically smell his elusive
quarry. Instinct? Or merely wishful thinking? Either
way, he felt charged, drunk with the heady scent of
blood, like some feral beast stalking its prey in ever-
narrowing circles.

"Zara..." His touch became firmer as he stroked

her sleep-warm face and urged her to open her eyes. "Come on, honey…time's a-wastin'."

She rolled onto her back and stretched languorously, ending on a deliciously carnal little grunt. Her eyes drifted open and she looked at him with a drowsy smile.

"Sleep well?" he asked.

Her gaze skipped down his bare torso and lower, to the scant towel held in place by little more than the clingy dampness of his skin. If she was embarrassed to see him in a state of dishabille, she hid it well.

Her voice was morning-husky, practically indecent. "Like a rock. Why is that, do you think?"

"Could be because you're exhausted, still recuperating. You should be home resting, not gallivanting around the state."

"I'm not gallivanting. I'm traipsing."

"Is there a difference?"

"Yeah, you want to know what it is?"

"Nope."

She pushed herself to a sitting position. "So what's on tap for the day? What do we do first?"

"What's this 'we' stuff, Kemo-sabe?"

"Oh, don't start! I'm in this, too."

He rose and started rummaging through his duffel lying open on the other bed. He'd brought extra clothes for both of them, though when she'd seen the color combination of the sleep ensemble he'd chosen—olive green undershirt paired with crimson satin boxers—she'd been less than thrilled.

He said, "I'll start at that bookstore, but something tells me I won't have much luck there."

She finger-combed her tousled hair. "You're hoping someone remembers Mac?"

"Yep." He pointed to his face. "Or recognizes him."

Her eyes brightened. "I hadn't thought of that."

He pulled out underwear, fresh jeans and a black polo shirt. "This is the closest I have at the moment to Mac's sartorial elegance. It'll have to do."

"He wears his hair loose."

"I know." He hooked a thumb under the towel and sent her a warning glance. "If your heart can't stand the shock of my naked stallionlike splendor, you'd better cover your eyes now."

Her lopsided grin was bewitching. "Stallionlike, huh? See, now you've gone and piqued my curiosity." She settled back to enjoy the show.

Logan whipped off the towel and tossed it on the bed.

And Zara looked. With simple appreciation and, yes, curiosity. Though there was nothing salacious in her regard, he felt the first stirrings of tumescence and made short work of stepping into his briefs.

"Did I lie?" he asked.

A slow smile. "Stallionlike. Is this where I twitch my tail and whinny like a mare in heat?"

So much for flaccidity. He quickly dragged his jeans over his hips and gave himself a little adjustment before zipping up. If this filly twitched her tail just once, he'd bar the stable doors and to hell with Abernathy Books.

He said, "If you want to come with me, you'd better get that tail moving."

Zara yawned hugely with a placating little wave

that failed to inspire confidence. He grabbed the damp towel and twirled it into a menacing corkscrew, advancing on her.

"I'm up!" She tossed off her covers and dashed into the bathroom, but failed to dodge his well-aimed fanny flick.

ABERNATHY BOOKS WAS a cozy, old-fashioned bookstore on the main drag in Hobart. The young saleswoman didn't recognize Logan, but the manager did. She asked how his mother had liked the Southwestern cookbook. He wasn't surprised by how open and friendly she seemed—his brother could be quite the charmer. A few subtle questions revealed she'd only seen Mac the once and had no clue as to where he might be staying.

He prayed the price sticker wasn't a false lead. It was possible Mac had simply been passing through when he stopped in Hobart to purchase the book. If so, they were back to square one.

They made their way through the sleepy town, moving from the hardware and video stores to the five-and-dime, supermarket, deli, fast-food places, service stations, restaurants and bank. No one recognized Logan's distinctive face. If Mac was in residence, he was keeping a low profile.

It took them the whole day to finally hit pay dirt. At Hobart Liquors the owner perked up when he spotted Logan and asked if he could get him his usual fifth of Absolut. They ascertained only that Mac had been a regular cash-and-carry customer for several weeks.

The pharmacist, too, recognized Logan and asked

if his busted ribs had healed. Gage would be pleased knowing he'd inflicted that much damage during their tussle. Like the liquor store, the pharmacy had never delivered anything to Mac's home, so there was no record of where he was staying. But at least now they knew he was local. And where Mac was, Candy and Emma most likely were, too.

In the early evening they found themselves at Mallory's Ale House discussing their progress over thick bacon burgers and waffle-cut Cajun fries. The pub offered fifty-six varieties of draft beer; they both chose an India pale ale.

Logan was relieved to see Zara's shoulders shimmy in delight at her first bite of the messy burger, appetite being a reliable barometer of health in his book.

He said, "Mac's probably renting a place under an assumed name."

"Can we lay a trap at your parents' house?"

"We could do that, but chances are it'll be days before he makes another appearance there. They said he visits only once a week—"

"And he was there just yesterday," she finished. "We can't delay that long, not when we might be so close now to where he's holding Mom and Emma...."

Logan took a long pull of the cold, deliciously bitter ale and leaned back. His plate was empty. Zara was still methodically plowing through her meal. He said, "You gonna finish that?"

"Yes, and I'm going to take my sweet time doing it, so hands off."

He hailed the waiter and ordered another pile of fries.

Zara took a delicate bite of the well-done burger—

Logan's had been blood-rare—and wiped her fingers on her napkin. "So far, we've taken sort of a scattershot approach, canvassing the local businesses."

"You have a better idea?"

"I don't know. Let's think about what in particular might lead us to your brother. What special needs does he have, no matter where he is?"

Logan thought about it. He shrugged. "Anyone with a home and car could have need of repair people. But the local service stations haven't done any work for him. And I can't see visiting every plumber and electrician within a twenty-mile radius."

She leaned forward on her elbows, her beautiful face screwed in concentration. "What's important to *Mac?* What can't he live without?"

Staring into Zara's eyes, he knew the instant the idea struck her—the same instant it struck him. "Computer!"

"You said he was really into computer games."

"He's addicted," he said. "I'll bet he spends a lot of time surfing the Net, too. There's no place to buy computers or software in Hobart, but we can check out the neighboring towns."

She picked up one of her Cajun fries and examined it contemplatively. "What if his machine went on the fritz?"

"He'd waste no time getting it fixed. Mac loves his computer games, but he's no expert on how the thing runs. He's always relied on outside people, not just for repairs but for technical advice, designing systems, you name it."

A silent communication arced between them, an

implicit agreement on their next plan of action. The young waiter arrived with the fries.

Logan said, "Do you guys have a computer here?"

"Sure. But the boss is happy with it, you know? I don't think he wants to upgrade if that's what you're—"

"No, I'm not in the business. I'm looking for a computer whiz—a consultant or repair guy. The hard drive in my laptop crashed."

The waiter's brow furrowed. "Lemme ask Joe. He knows about this stuff." He circled the brick half wall separating the dining portion of the pub from the bar, where several tall, decorative beer taps stood sentry. After a brief confab with the bartender, he returned with a name and phone number scrawled on a cocktail napkin.

"Joe says this guy's the best propeller head in the area. Everyone around here uses him."

"Barry Geffler," Logan read. "Can I use your phone?"

"I guess so. It's behind the bar."

Logan dialed the number on the napkin and listened to the phone on the other end ring and ring. He pictured the nerdy "propeller head" hunched over a state-of-the-art computer in some cluttered little room, tweaking and customizing hardware and software for his clients.

Geffler finally picked up on the twelfth ring. Logan explained he had a problem with his laptop and needed immediate help.

"I can give you, like, Friday morning."

"And I can give you two hundred bucks cash if you're at Mallory's within fifteen minutes."

"Order me a Watney's stout."

Click.

Twelve and a half minutes later a tall young man sauntered through the door and scanned the sparsely populated pub. He was in his early twenties, with thick sun-streaked hair, electric blue eyes and a day's growth of whiskers on the kind of jaw usually associated with the word *chiseled.* His athletic build was displayed to advantage in a brown leather jacket and snug black jeans. A motorcycle helmet was tucked under one arm.

"Think that's him?" Zara whispered, eyeing the guy up and down.

Her voice had a mildly breathless quality that Logan found irksome. He started to say, "You've got to be kidding," when the newcomer spotted him and waved. He strode toward their booth.

"Hey! How ya been, man?"

Logan automatically shook the proffered hand.

The young man offered Zara a brilliant smile, which she returned. "Barry Geffler. I did some computer work for Logan here a while back."

Logan? Was that Mac's idea of a joke, using his detested brother's name, or was it just one more symptom of his long-standing jealousy?

Zara appeared momentarily nonplussed as she introduced herself and offered her hand.

Barry turned to Logan. "Any more problems with your sound card?"

"Nope."

"Cool. Listen." Barry checked his intricate digital watch. "I don't wanna be rude or anything, but I've gotta meet a guy here within the next two minutes and nineteen sec—"

"Sit down." Logan shoved Barry's glass of beer across the scarred wooden table and slapped four fifties next to it. "I called you."

"Whoa. Why didn't you say it was you on the phone, man?" He slid onto the hard wooden bench and exchanged another dazzling smile with Zara, who scooted over to make room for him.

This was the local computer geek?

Logan said, "Barry, I'm going to ask you some questions that will seem very strange. Answer them anyway."

He shrugged and lifted his beer. "Fire away."

"What's my full name?"

Barry stared at him over the rim of the glass. He glanced at Zara before answering, "Logan Smith. Least, that's what you told me."

"I assume you came to my home to do this work…?"

A wary "Yeah…"

"When?"

"Uh…about three weeks ago, wasn't it?"

That was before Mac kidnapped Candy.

"Where do I live?" Logan was close, so close. He could taste it.

A slow grin spread across Barry's handsome face. "Come on, man. What's this about?"

Zara smiled sweetly. "I'd really like you to answer his question, Barry." She gave his leather-clad arm a gentle squeeze.

Logan sent her a quelling look, the one where he tilted his head down a fraction and glared menacingly from under his brows. Subtle but usually spectacularly effective. She just turned that sweet smile on him.

Barry eyed them warily. "I don't know.... This is too weird."

Logan snapped two more fifties out of his wallet and held them up.

"River Road." Barry's pupils dilated as he stared at the money. "You're renting the old MacAllen place."

Zara said, "Which is where exactly?"

"On the north side of the road. It's the only house between Harrison and McKinley. It's, like, isolated."

Logan asked, "Is there a street address?"

Barry shrugged. "Beats me. It's just the old MacAllen place, you know? Well, *you* know."

Logan tossed the fifties at him and surged to his feet.

"Hey!" Barry scooped up the cash. "Don't you want to know anything else? Ask me what kind of car you drive. How much RAM your laptop has."

The only question left was one none of them could answer.

Is it too late for Candy and Emma?

Chapter Twelve

Zara sat on the edge of the motel bed, watching Logan check his weapon and spare magazines. Suddenly this thing was too real, too *now*, her family's fate too precarious. What if Mac panicked and killed them? Didn't Logan say he could panic—

"Did you hear what I said?" Logan was watching her.

She licked her dry lips. "Sorry."

He laid the gun on the dresser and sat opposite her on the other bed, his knees bracketing hers. He took her icy hands in his big, warm ones and stared down at them, rubbing them with his thumbs. He looked at her, searched her eyes.

"Trust me, Zara."

She nodded automatically, her throat too tight for speech.

He squeezed her hands. "I mean *really* trust me. I intend to end this thing. Tonight."

He had to feel the fine tremors coursing through her, into her fingertips. "I guess I thought...I thought I was stronger than this. I fooled myself." She tried to smile. "One of my many talents."

He leaned forward slowly. Placed a soft kiss on her forehead. "You're so hard on yourself. Why are you so hard on yourself?"

She couldn't meet his eyes. "Logan…will you just hold me? Please?"

He pulled her onto his bed and stretched out next to her, one long arm circling her back. She tugged off her sling-back heels and tossed them over the side. Reaching over her to the night table, he switched off the light, swaddling them in a comforting gloom that seemed to amplify the distant sounds of traffic. She curled into him, slid her arm over his waist. He felt big and solid and indestructible.

The thought came to her again. If anyone could bring her mother and sister home, it was this man.

The warm masculine scent of him had long since burned itself into her subconscious, acting as a tranquilizer, a balm to her frazzled psyche. She breathed deeply and let her eyes drift shut.

She felt her body begin to relax, her heart rate to slow. She'd allow herself this, these few precious moments of serenity. She'd let herself pretend that everything was all right. Just for a few moments.

She mumbled, "I'm gonna fall asleep."

"Go ahead. I'll try not to wake you when I leave."

Her eyes snapped open. Her eyelashes brushed his shirt as she blinked. "I'm going with you, Logan."

He laughed. "Go to sleep."

She tried to lever herself up and look at him, but it was dark and she could barely make out the amber glint of his eyes. Before she could state her case, he said, "You're staying here, Zara. This is not negotiable."

Restraining her objections, she settled back into his arms, knowing she had no choice but to back down. For the moment.

His hand stroked her back in a slow, soothing rhythm. Unconsciously she burrowed closer to him, pressed her cheek to his steady heartbeat and let her legs twine with his.

She took comfort in the intimacy of their embrace, even as she acknowledged her body's first glimmerings of arousal. Along with the novelty of the sensation came grim resignation. This wasn't for her. Not anymore.

His fingertips skimmed her face, observing her as a blind man might, his touch light but thorough. His deep voice rumbled through her. "You're sad. Tell me why."

This man was more attuned to her feelings after six days than her ex-husband had been after six years.

She said, "I want what I can't have."

He sighed into her hair. His arms tightened fractionally. "We all want something we can't have, Zara. That doesn't keep us from trying. It's what makes us human."

"What do you want that you can't have?"

He stroked her hair. Pressed a kiss to the crown of her head. "I'd have to say…I want a part of me back that I've lost."

Her eyes brimmed with sudden tears. That was exactly how she felt. She didn't care that her voice betrayed her emotion. "What have you lost, Logan?"

"The piece of me that…" He seemed to be searching for the words. "That shouldn't belong to me at all, but to someone else. The part of me I should be able to give away. I'm not saying this very well."

"You're saying it just fine."

He was telling her he couldn't love. She felt his sense of loss. It mirrored her own. Whatever he'd been through that had made him feel this way, she wished he'd share it. But she knew she couldn't ask him to trust her with his pain; it would have to come from him.

He said, "Tell me what you want. What you think you can't have."

She murmured, "I think you know."

After a few moments he said, "You don't feel…whole. Because someone hurt you."

Whole. She'd never thought about it in just that way, but now that he'd said it, she knew it was true. She hadn't felt whole in a long time.

Last night he'd said if she wanted to talk about it, he wanted to listen. He wouldn't ask her again. *Who hurt you?* God knew she didn't want to talk about it, had never talked about it, but suddenly she did want him to understand.

She whispered, "It was Tony."

She felt his heart thud faster. He waited. Waited for her to say it. Suddenly she wished desperately that he would say it for her. He had to know.

She choked on the words. "He raped me."

His arms crushed her. A wrenching sob tore up through her, rising on a swell of anger and shame. "He *raped* me, Logan."

She couldn't breathe for the tears choking her. She was shocked by the overwhelming magnitude of her anguish, chagrined that Logan was witness to it. But through it all he held her, so tight she melted into him. He stroked her hair, murmured in her ear, urging her to let it out.

At length her grief wound down. She gulped great, shuddering breaths, her face still pressed to his shirt, soaked with her tears.

He reached across her again to grab a handful of tissues. She wiped her face and blew her nose and tossed the wadded tissues in the general direction of the wastebasket. Her face felt hot, her eyes puffy. Inside, she felt lighter, as if the tears she'd released had been in there all along, weighing her down.

At last Logan said, "When did this happen?"

"At the end, when he was served with divorce papers. I don't think he ever expected me to take the initiative and leave him. He was outraged. He wanted to hurt me. Debase me. So he did."

"And you never told anyone?"

"No. I was too ashamed. I pulled myself together, covered the bruises with makeup. No one knew."

"Zara." He cupped her face, as if trying to read her expression in the dark. "I know you're too smart to blame yourself for what he did to you."

"It's not that I blame myself. It's not that. It's just…I knew I'd failed him. As a wife. What kind of wife makes a man want to do something like that?"

She sensed Logan's frustration. He paused as if struggling to find the right words. "You said it yourself, Zara. He attacked you because he wanted to hurt you. Don't you see? It wasn't about you. It was about *him,* and his twisted ego. No failure on your part, no matter how much you think you may have let him down, made him do what he did. Nothing justifies it."

"I—I know that, it's just…"

"The guy spent six years belittling you, convincing you you're worthless." He shook his head, his voice tinged with disgust. "He and your old man, what a pair. It's like I said before. They were a couple of control freaks, threatened by your independence, your competence. Deep down, I'm sure they knew you didn't need them. Would've been better off *without* them."

"Logan, you've only known me a few days," she observed sadly, "and you've only heard my side of things. Dad and Tony lived with me for years. You don't think maybe they knew me a little better than you do…?"

He leaned up on an elbow; she felt his tension. "You tell me, Zara. Did Tony know you? Did he know when you needed an encouraging word, someone to listen to your frustrations and your fears? Did he know when you needed him to praise your accomplishments, support your decisions?"

His words stunned her into silence. He was describing the perfect *wife*, the ideal, nurturing partner she'd tried to be. As liberated as she thought she was, she'd never associated that kind of emotional sustenance with a husband's role.

Not that she was an expert on husbands' and wives' roles. Her early exposure to the institution of marriage had presented a distorted picture at best. She'd been raised in a broken home, presided over by a cold, authoritarian father who'd ruthlessly separated his infant daughters from the mother they'd needed.

The truth was, Logan did know her better than either her father or her husband had. Hadn't she just marveled at how attuned he was to her emotions? Logan saw inside her…and, incredibly, he liked what he saw. He believed in her goodness.

His quiet voice broke into her thoughts. "Answer me, Zara. Did Tony really know you?"

"No." The admission was as liberating as it was depressing. "No, he never knew me."

"And neither did your father. And all those spiteful things they said about you…?"

She laughed. This sweet, stubborn man actually had her laughing! "A vicious crock of lies."

"There! I knew you'd figure it out."

"Yeah, perceptive little ole me."

She sensed his smile even before she lifted her fingers to explore his face as he'd explored hers earlier. She felt the fan of crinkles at the corner of his eye, the furrows bracketing his mouth. His lips responded to her touch, closing gently over a fingertip.

The dark magnified everything: the feel of his lips, supple and greedy, drawing her finger into his hot mouth; the tantalizing scrape of sharp teeth, in startling contrast to the velvet stroke of his strong, lively tongue; the rhythmic suction that urged her to respond.

She gave in to his silent command and moved her finger to the cadence he set. Such a simple act, yet so blatantly sexual.

Her soft moan triggered an immediate response. He jerked her hand away and hauled her close, his mouth finding hers with unerring precision in the dark. He kissed her urgently, hungrily, holding her tight, squeezing the air from her lungs. But she didn't need air, she only needed this voracious mouth, this silky tongue stabbing deep and hard until her very insides clutched at the hot, stroking length of it.

At last he broke off, panting. "Zara…what you do to me…" She lay clinging to him, trembling, struggling to make her brain function. Still holding her, he dropped his head to the pillow, clearly fighting for control. "I guess a cold shower is in order."

He let his words hang there as silence stretched between them. She knew what he was waiting for. It was her call. She'd have to make the next move. He wouldn't push her. She wanted him so badly it hurt, yet with each passing second, her courage slipped a notch.

Both her father and her husband had found her sadly lacking. Yet here was this remarkable man who saw qualities in her they never had, qualities she herself hadn't known were there. The prospect of disappointing him terrified her. She lay still and mute, paralyzed by her cowardice and the old insecurities.

After a minute he started to ease away from her. She stopped him with a light touch. And swallowed hard, her throat suddenly dry.

"Don't," she whispered.

He sat still, waiting. When she said nothing more he slid an arm around her and urged her to lie with him again, curled against his side.

He said quietly, "I want you to know, I can be very gentle."

The simple declaration, obviously meant to calm her, instead sent her pulse into overdrive. But why? *Gentle* certainly had no place in the fantasy her unruly imagination had concocted these last few days, a fantasy featuring Logan Byrne as the energetic, inventive lover instinct told her he was. He'd already demonstrated his sexually assertive nature, and she'd be lying if she claimed it didn't excite her. That excitement was due in part to the fact that she felt safe with Logan; she knew he'd never cross the line into unwanted aggression.

Yet somehow, she found his soft-spoken reassurance just as exciting. This vigorous, virile man was ready to rein in his natural impulses by sheer force of will, summoning all his tenderness and patience for her sake. Not the seduction she'd fantasized, but potent stuff in its own right.

His hand glided across her shoulder to the collar of her soft rayon blouse, half of a calf-length two-piece dress. His movements were so leisurely she didn't notice he was working the buttons free until she felt cool air whisper between her breasts. Her breath caught.

"Do you want me to stop?" His tone was so casual he could have been talking about the weather. She didn't answer. He started rebuttoning her blouse.

"No!" she rasped.

His nimble fingers returned to their task. She lay on her side, perfectly still, feeling her heartbeat quicken with every button he released. When he reached the waistband of her skirt, he tugged out the tails of the blouse.

With maddening nonchalance he flicked the fabric aside and ran his hand lightly over her breasts, cleavaged to the max by her side-lounging position. He ran a fingertip along the lace of her bra. "What color is this?"

Her voice was hoarse. "Red. You packed it."

"Oh yeah, I did. I like red."

He eased first one arm out of the blouse, then the other. He unclasped her bra and drew it off her, his attitude composed, almost indifferent.

"Logan…?" She hadn't said yes yet, didn't know if she could. What was he doing?

"Stay here."

She felt the mattress dip as he rose and crossed the room. The bathroom light flicked on. After a few moments his large form reappeared, silhouetted in the bathroom doorway. He kicked off his sneakers before joining her on the bed once more. He sat cross-legged, and in the meager light washing in from the bathroom she saw him uncap a tiny plastic bottle—one of the toiletry samples left for motel guests.

He held the open bottle under her nose. "Lotion." She sniffed the light floral scent.

"You're very tense," he said, pushing on her shoulder, urging her onto her stomach. "When was the last time you had a back rub?" He lifted her arms from her sides, and she folded them under her head.

"When I could still afford it, before the divorce."

"A back rub's like sex—not the same if you have to pay for it."

He levered himself over her with pure masculine grace to straddle her buttocks. He kept his weight off her, but still she was acutely aware of his heat, where his sinewy, denim-clad thighs touched her hips.

He placed the bottle on the night table, and she heard a wet sound as he warmed some of the lotion in his hands.

"Relax," he said. "You're stiff as a board."

She took a deep breath and willed the tension from her body. Nevertheless, his first touch made her jump.

His warm, slick hands glided over her skin. Splayed, they felt huge, practically covering her entire back. He pushed them from her waist slowly up to her shoulders. A little sigh escaped her. Her elderly Austrian masseuse had never had hands like these.

His long, strong fingers kneaded the tight muscles at the base of her neck, turning them to jelly before moving on to her shoulders.

She moaned, feeling herself begin to relax. "Mmm, you are good at this."

"I'm good at everything I do, Zara."

She smirked at the not-so-subtle implication. His thumbs worked their way up her spine, molding the flesh on either side of it. He worked methodically, isolating muscle groups, pressing and stroking until she lay limp as a rag.

He warmed more lotion and worked on her sides, starting at her waist and moving upward. When he reached the sides of her breasts, pressed against the quilted bedspread, he didn't hesitate but massaged them, too, while his thumbs rubbed her shoulder blades. Feeling ridiculously tranquil, she basked in the pampering ministrations of those long, slippery fingers—and in the faint hum of awareness resonating from somewhere deep within her.

At some point her sluggish mind registered the subtle change as pure relaxation gave way to a sensual lethargy.

He finished with light, sweeping strokes of her back. "Turn over."

She roused herself to obey, peering up at him

through half-open lids as he once again lifted her arms over her head. His dark hair lay loose around his shoulders. His eyes were unreadable in the dim light, but held an underlying intensity that raised her listless pulse just a fraction.

He palmed more lotion and began at her waist, smoothing his hands over her abdomen, stroking outward, applying just the right amount of pressure. She watched him, watched the muscles of his shoulders bunch and relax under the black polo shirt. Maintaining the same indolent pace, he worked on her rib cage. His hands skated up her sides to her shoulders and upper arms, giving each area special attention.

He moved on to her chest, kneading those muscles, lifting and massaging her breasts as he did so. His expression never changed.

That hum of awareness within her rose in pitch and volume. She wondered vaguely if he could hear it, feel it. His hands glided outward across her chest, and she felt her peaked nipples scrape his palms. Her eyes closed on a faint whimper. They slowly drifted open and she saw him watching her face, studying her.

He swept his hands down her torso and up again, gave her shoulders one last firm stroke and sat back on his heels.

"Better?" he asked, swinging his leg over her, dismounting.

Her response was an inarticulate grunt. *Yes. No. Don't stop.*

She knew she should be embarrassed by her obvious arousal—the stiff peaks of her breasts, the flush that warmed her face and chest—but she was too relaxed to care. And somehow she knew that with this man, she had nothing to feel embarrassed about.

For the first time in years, she welcomed the yearning, luxuriated in the little signs heralding the excitement building within her. For the first time in years, she took joy in her rising passion.

He settled on his side, propped on an elbow. "I don't have to stop. I think there are still a few pockets of tension left." He slid a hand up one stocking-clad shin and under the hem of her long, loose skirt. She felt it glide upward between her thighs, and gasped as his hot fingers met the bare skin above the tops of her stockings. It was too intense. She quivered like a bowstring, pressing her legs together.

"See?" he said, letting his hand linger there, a hairbreadth from the seat of her desire. "You're still tense."

She managed to croak, "You're a very wicked man."

He looked devastatingly handsome with that arrogant grin and those sparking golden eyes. "Now you've gone and hurt my feelings." He moved his fingers, stroking the sensitive insides of her thighs. "How do you propose to make it up to me?"

She chuckled. "Very, very wicked..."

His fingers slid upward a fraction to skim the silk of her panties. The sharp buzz of sensation there, *right there,* galvanized her, lifting her hips off the bed. Automatically she started to reach for his wrist, then dropped her hand.

No. She didn't want to stop him. She knew that now.

He smiled gently. He saw it all, she could tell: her internal struggle, her implicit answer.

Yes.

He gave her thigh a little squeeze and withdrew his hand. "Where does this open?" He searched the waistband and found the side button. Within seconds she lay there in only her red satin thong panties, matching garter belt and sheer black stockings.

"I've fantasized about seeing you in these things for too damn long." Taking her hand, he wordlessly invited her to stand up and model for him.

She willingly did so, reveling in the look in his eyes, in the knowledge that she was desired, in her ability to strip away this man's civilized veneer and expose the snorting, pawing, howling beast within.

He said, "Turn around."

She did—and wished she could still see his expression, knowing what he was looking at: her bare back and nearly bare bottom, its very nakedness enhanced by the slim thong and the garter straps hooked to her stockings.

As she stood there for what seemed an eternity, she began to comprehend what all the fuss was about, why Logan had assumed her lingerie collection had been purchased by a man. She'd never felt more alluring.

He touched her bottom and she drew in a sharp breath. Her muscles jumped under his lightly stroking fingers. He moved on to her hips, her back.

His breath was hot on her neck as his hands came around to cover her breasts. "Have I ever told you how very beautiful you are?"

"I—I think you have."

"Well, I can't say it enough. You have an effect on me that's practically illegal." He turned her and pulled her into his arms, and she felt the illegal effect immediately, prodding her belly through his jeans.

He tipped her head back and took her mouth with all the eagerness and impatience she herself felt. He nibbled her lips, sucked on them, tasted them thoroughly before deepening the kiss.

She shuddered as his tongue slid past her lips. He held her tighter, crushing her breasts against his shirt. Before Logan, she had never appreciated this kind of kiss, but now she understood what that fuss, too, was about. She couldn't restrain herself and didn't try.

He groaned as she responded in kind, timidly at first. The tip of her tongue touched smooth, even teeth. It flicked over the pointed crest of a canine, and she shivered at the feral images that came to mind. His tongue engaged hers in a primitive mating, until they had to break off for air. He pressed fast, moist, dizzying kisses to her face, to her cheeks and eyelids and temples. If he hadn't been holding her, her legs would have buckled.

"Tell me what you want me to do," he said. "What do you like?"

She experienced a flash of panic, feeling woefully unsophisticated, a fraud. "I—I don't know." When had it ever mattered what she liked?

"I know your breasts are very sensitive. Do you like this?" he murmured, caressing her with feathery, teasing strokes. He ran his thumb around the peak of one breast, watching it tighten further. A desperate little sigh escaped her. "I think that was a yes."

He leaned down. His humid breath curled over her

breasts as he murmured, "And this?" He placed a soft kiss on one aching tip. Her knees wobbled.

"Logan…" she groaned.

"Do you like it?" he persisted.

"Yes. *Yes!*"

He sucked the nipple deep into his mouth, and her legs gave out. Scooping her into his arms, he deposited her diagonally across the bed. She writhed as he suckled and caressed her, holding fast to him, tangling her fingers in his long hair.

He seized her mouth in a hard, savage kiss as he parted her legs and fitted himself against her. She grasped his buttocks and arched into him, the pressure of his arousal tantalizing, maddening. If not for the barrier of their clothing, he'd be inside her.

And every nerve, every quivering synapse, screamed for him to be inside her.

Abruptly he lunged across her and upended his duffel on the other bed. He found the string of condoms, tossed them on the night table and yanked off his shirt.

Zara found his stampeding urgency immensely arousing. Kneeling on the bed, she reached for his belt buckle and slid leather through brass with trembling fingers. She dragged open his bulging zipper and closed her hand over his penis through his briefs. He twitched and pulsed under her fingers.

His harsh sigh sounded almost pained. He stood very still, muscles tensed. She began to tug his jeans over his hips, but he lost patience with her slow progress and commandeered the job. In seconds he was nude.

The urge to touch him was overpowering. She ran

her hands over his corrugated belly and the lean, hard muscles of his hips and thighs. His heavy erection nodded from its thicket of dark hair.

She felt raw, remade, as if her hurtful past had been wiped clean and she were discovering her womanhood—her birthright—for the very first time. Tears of joy stung her eyes. She pressed a tender kiss to Logan's chest. He cradled her head in those huge, capable hands.

"Zara?" Frowning, he lifted her chin. "Are you crying? Did I upset—"

"No. No, I'm...happy."

His expression softened. He brushed his thumb across her mouth. "There hasn't been anyone since Tony, has there?"

"No."

"I won't do anything you don't want me to do. You can stop me at any time." He offered a lopsided smile. "It'll kill me, but you can do it."

"I know that."

He leaned down and kissed her, almost chastely. Hooking his fingers in her panties, he tugged them halfway down her thighs, until her garter hooks got in the way. He scowled at this unforeseen dilemma, clearly unaccustomed to old-fashioned stockings.

Before she could unhook her garters, the professional problem solver reached for his jeans and extracted a small penknife from a pocket. He flipped it open. "Hold still."

She watched wide-eyed as he slit the sides of her panties, folded the knife and tossed it and her ruined thong on the pile of clothing.

"I'll buy you another one."

"Don't worry about it," she said breathlessly as he gently pushed her onto her back. Her legs hung over the side of the bed, and he knelt on the carpet between them. Her heart thumped in anticipation.

He skimmed his hands up her thighs and brushed his thumbs through the dark tangle of hair. She wondered, could he see it, her body's hungry, grasping response? Exerting subtle pressure, he parted her, opened her to his avid gaze.

She clutched the bedspread in white-knuckled fists, her hips rocking of their own accord, imploringly. When his mouth touched her there she screamed. With his fingers and lips and strong, lithe tongue he quickly brought her to the razor's edge of release and held her there, teasing, backing off, teasing again.

She thrashed beneath him, sobbing her pleasure, unencumbered by pride or modesty, overwhelmed by the sheer joy of sharing herself with this man.

He broke away to tear a packet off the string of condoms. A heartbeat later he was kneeling before her once more, pulling her closer and holding her legs wide. His eyes held her spellbound, never straying from hers, as he filled her in one slow, deep thrust, a leisurely penetration she felt in every cell of her body.

His thick, unyielding length opened her, stretched her almost to the point of pain. She wrapped her legs around his waist, her panting breaths punctuated by sharp little cries of pleasure.

His eyes closed as he pressed home the final distance, flexing into her. She felt her climax begin to crest, amorphous filaments of pure sensation fusing, gelling, even as he lingered within her, motionless.

Still staring at him, she smiled at the pure wonder

of what was about to happen. "Logan," she whimpered, "hold me!" Without his strong arms grounding her, she'd surely fly apart.

But he already knew, just by watching her face. Already he was gathering her to him, holding her tight. Her rock, her anchor. His first tiny movement spurred her orgasm. It burst within her, rocked her off the bed, a white-hot firebomb of pure light and energy.

He drove into her, fast and fierce, stoking the flame, making it burn hotter, brighter. He tilted her hips, altered the angle and cadence of his thrusts, prolonging her release.

She clung to him in the aftermath, panting, trembling, laughing breathlessly. His answering grin was part affection, part pure masculine conceit as he brushed strands of damp hair off her forehead. She knew he was exerting immense control, balanced on the high wire of his own climax. She felt him everywhere inside her at once, a rigid, throbbing presence that nudged the very heart of her.

Pushing up on her arms, she wriggled off the bed and onto his lap, still joined with him. She kissed him, delicate nipping kisses, and began to move once more.

"Zara!" He gripped her hips hard, holding her still. "Not yet..." In the same breath he growled, "Oh, hell."

He plunged and retreated without restraint, guiding her movements. In the end he rammed her against the side of the bed and came with a savage cry.

Zara knew she'd never seen anything as beautiful as Logan's face when he toppled from the high wire.

Chapter Thirteen

Zara slipped her shoes on, watching Logan get ready to leave for Mac's place. He donned his shoulder holster and pulled his hair back in his usual ponytail. Shrugging into his black windbreaker, he said, "I'll be back in a minute. Have to get something from the car."

He stepped out, and she allowed herself a little smile of triumph. He hadn't said a word when, instead of curling up and falling asleep after their exhaustive lovemaking, she'd gotten dressed. She took that as a hopeful sign that he'd changed his mind about letting her come along. She hadn't mentioned it, though, preferring not to press her luck.

When one minute turned to five, then ten, she realized he'd been gone too long. Had he skipped out on her? His BMW was parked in front of their room. Surely she would have heard him drive away. She was halfway to the window when the muffled thunk of the car's trunk sounded, followed moments later by the rasp of his key in the door.

He entered carrying a small satchel, which he

dropped on a little writing table in a corner of the room.

She asked, "That took long enough. What did you get?"

"Come here. We need to talk." He swung the straight chair away from the table.

Uh-oh. She approached slowly, marshaling her arguments, all the rational reasons she should accompany him. First and foremost, she was terrified for Logan's safety. What if he needed backup? He had an extra gun for her, she was sure. And what if Candy or Emma was hurt and needed her?

"Logan—"

"Sit down." He patted the chair and moved behind it to open the satchel.

She sat. "I want you to listen to me before you make a— What are you doing?"

He'd pulled her arms behind the chair back. She felt something wind around her wrists.

Rope!

He was tying her up!

"*Logan!*"

"Don't fuss. You'll hurt yourself." He deftly knotted the nylon cord. It was just tight enough to hold her securely without impeding circulation.

She kicked wildly as he squatted in front of her and reached for a leg. "Ow!" he yelped. "Damn!" He yanked off her delicate high-heeled sling-backs and stared at the things as if they were some diabolical new weapon. Tossing them aside, he made short work of securing her ankles to the front chair legs.

She was speechless, trembling with rage. He arranged her long skirt demurely over her knees. "I know you, Zara. The minute I took off, you'd call a cab and follow me.''

Well, of course she would.

He continued, "I told you before, I'm not willing to endanger you.''

"You—you're just going to leave me here like this? Tied up? *Helpless?*''

"Only until I return.'' He stood up. "And if I don't make it back—''

"No!'' she cried. "Don't say that.'' She couldn't bear the thought of Logan being hurt—or worse. Especially after what they'd just shared. Her eyes burned, but she refused to shed one tear. She had to keep her wits.

He sighed. "We both know the risks, Zara. That's why I stopped in the motel office just now. Arranged for a baby-sitter for you.''

"A *what!*''

"Lucky for us, the assistant manager's just getting off work.''

A knock on the door startled her. Logan crossed the room in three long strides and ushered in Bette Davis. This was Bette in her scary later pictures, squirrelly and pop-eyed.

The woman took two steps into the room and stopped dead in her tracks, staring at Zara bound to the chair. Logan closed the door and whipped out his bogus FBI badge. He wagged it in her face to snag her attention.

"Special Agent Logan Pierce.'' He gravely intoned, "Mrs. Feeney, the FBI needs your help.''

Zara muttered, "Oh, brother.''

He snapped the badge wallet shut and was about

to return it to his pocket when Mrs. Feeney's sand-paper voice stopped him.

"Not so fast. Lemme see that again." She plucked a pair of reading glasses from a canvas tote bag filled to overflowing with skeins of yarn in pastel shades. Sliding them onto her nose, she scrutinized the ID.

Zara said, "Logan, this is pathetic."

He ignored her. "Mrs. Feeney, the Bureau occasionally must enlist the aid of concerned citizens such as yourself. This is one such time. I need you to guard this prisoner for a few hours while I'm gone."

She handed back the badge. "What'd she do?"

"You don't recognize her?"

She studied Zara. "Should I?"

"Don't you watch 'Unsolved Crimes'?"

"Good grief!" Zara jerked at her restraints. "Stop wasting this poor woman's time, Logan. *Let me go!*"

Mrs. Feeney answered, "I try to catch it, but my craft group meets on Sundays."

Folding his arms, Logan jerked his head toward Zara. "This one was featured a few weeks ago. She and her gang have robbed twenty-three banks across the Northeast. I just caught up with her—she was about to knock over Hobart Savings Bank."

Mrs. Feeney's eyes bulged alarmingly. "My nephew works in that bank!"

Zara moaned, "I don't believe this."

He said, "I was transporting her to prison when I got news of a kidnapping nearby."

"That's true!" Zara said. "That last part's true! It's my mother and my twin sister who've been kidnapped, by *his* twin brother, and he's just doing this so I can't follow him and help to free them! *And.*"

She hopped forward a little in her chair. "He isn't really an FBI agent, Mrs. Feeney! That badge is *fake!*"

Mrs. Feeney stared at her as if she'd sprouted a third eye.

Logan shook his head sadly. "Pitiful, isn't it? I've seen this before. When the law catches up to them, they go kind of nuts, spouting the first crazy thing that pops into their heads. You'd never think, looking at her now, that she's killed three bank guards in cold blood, would you?"

"No," Mrs. Feeney said. "I wouldn't."

"I'm going to leave you with this, in case she manages to get free." He pulled a hefty black revolver out of the satchel. Zara and the assistant manager both gasped. "Have you ever used a gun, Mrs. Feeney?"

"God, no!"

"It's very simple." He drew a bead on Zara, two-handed. "You just aim, like this, and pull the trigger. See? Nothing to it."

"Don't you have to cock it first?"

"That's a very good question. Nowadays all revolvers are double-action. Like this one, which happens to be a .357 Magnum."

"Oh my."

"You can cock it if you want to—like this—and that makes the trigger more sensitive, easier to pull. Or you can just shoot without cocking it, in which case it'll take a little more effort to pull the trigger. But watch out—this weapon has quite a kick."

He handed the gun to Mrs. Feeney, who practiced pointing it at her bound prisoner, squinting over the top of her reading glasses. The gun wobbled as her finger groped for the trigger pull.

Logan chuckled. "Easy now, you don't want to shoot her just yet."

"Oh!" She giggled sheepishly, one hand fluttering at her chest. "No. Not yet."

"Hel-*lo-o*," Zara said. "Have you lost your *mind*, Logan? You're not really going to run off and leave me at the mercy of Baby Jane here?"

Mrs. Feeney said, "Young lady, we'll get along just fine if you can manage to behave yourself."

"Logan!"

He turned to Mrs. Feeney. "If she gets loud, or you get tired of listening to her rantings, feel free to gag her. Now, this part is important." He scribbled something on the scratch pad next to the phone. "If I'm not back by 2:00 a.m., call this number and ask for Lou."

"What do I tell him?"

Zara shouted, *"Her.* It's Lou*ise!* You tell her her good buddy Logan's gone off the deep end! You tell her *Zara's going to rip his damn heart out when she gets free!"*

Mrs. Feeney scowled down at her. "I have had just about enough of that mouth of yours, missy. You've brought this all on yourself, you know."

He told Mrs. Feeney, "If you have to call Lou, you just tell her everything I told you, and follow her instructions."

Baby Jane settled on a stuffed chair with her knitting and her firearm. Logan paused in the doorway, answering Zara's murderous glare with a disarming wink. "I can tell you two are going to get along just fine."

THE WINDOWS at the front of the house glowed. From his hiding place fifty feet away behind a huge oak tree, Logan watched a shadow move behind sheer curtains.

Mac.

He'd done reconnaissance when he'd first arrived, cautiously circling the huge Tudor-style house with his small flashlight, checking out the doors and windows. He'd identified the louvered basement window as being the best place to break in. It wasn't wired to the security system as were the other windows, but was boarded from the inside. Also, it was located at the rear of the house. If Mac remained in the front room, chances were he wouldn't hear Logan enter.

He was about to head around back when the sound of car tires on gravel arrested him.

"Damn."

Moonlight glinted off a sleek gray Mercedes, rolling to a stop on the circular driveway. When the driver's door opened, the interior light illuminated an older man, trim and well dressed, early to mid-sixties. Using an elegant brass-tipped cane for leverage, he eased out of the car. As his shadowed form made its way up the walk and the front steps, Logan detected a pronounced limp.

Frustration surged within him, but he tamped it down with the discipline he'd spent fifteen years honing. Emotions compromised one's perspective. He'd wait, watch, adapt.

But as he'd told Zara, he intended to end this thing tonight.

The front door swung open and Logan got his first clear look at his brother. Mac stood in the entryway, drink in hand. He appeared surprised to see his visitor, then angry.

The older man held his own, practically shoving his way into the house, despite his handicap. Mac slammed the door after him.

Logan crept closer, risking a move into the open, knowing his brother was distracted at the moment by his unwelcome guest. Silently he gained the house and stepped over shrubs to take up position near the half-open living room window. Heated voices drifted to him.

"...deadline's tomorrow, William."

"Did you think I'd fork over eight million without even seeing her for myself?"

"How'd you find me?"

The breeze fluttered the curtains, and Logan got glimpses of the two men. The visitor, William, stood straight and dignified, one powerful-looking fist clenching the head of his cane. His wavy hair was steel gray, his thick eyebrows black. Intense gray-green eyes followed Mac's agitated pacing.

William's voice was deep and assertive. "You've underestimated my resources."

Mac sneered. "These the same 'resources' that'll make me sorry if something happens to your beloved scream queen?"

"The very ones. And the same goes for the daughters, too, as we discussed on Monday."

It was a clash of wills, Logan realized, between two

bullheaded men, neither of whom was accustomed to being thwarted. This William had to be the bucks behind the theft of the ray gun. What was his interest in Candy Carmelle? Why was he willing to pay that kind of money for her? If he were simply some wealthy crackpot collector, he wouldn't be so concerned with the safety of Candy and her daughters. There had to be some history here.

Mac asked, "Do you have the money?"

"I have the money." Through the gap in the curtains Logan saw William's cold smile. "Not on me, of course. I may be obsessed, as you put it, but I'm no fool. Where is she?"

Mac stared at him, and Logan could almost hear the gears turning in his twin brother's head. How far should he cooperate, how much leverage did he have, how much of William's threats was bluster?

Eight million was at stake, if he'd heard correctly. Logan grimaced. The going price for a well-preserved former starlet.

Finally Mac said, "I'll get her. You wait here." He headed toward the back of the house.

Left alone, William seemed to lose some of his starch. He leaned heavily on his cane, looking almost haggard, as if the worry and remorse Logan saw etched on his features were as crippling as his disability. When footsteps sounded, he snapped upright, his expression once more stony and forbidding.

Mac hauled Candy into the room with a brutal grip on her upper arm. She looked rumpled but intact, with an undeniable spirit behind the dark eyes that reminded Logan of her daughters.

Candy's defiant expression changed the instant she

laid eyes on William. Logan was right. There was history here, in spades. Her gaze held enough love, longing and regret for a lifetime.

William barked, "Release her!"

Mac hesitated an instant, then obeyed, giving her a little shove. William and Candy stared at each other. Logan sensed a deep connection between these two. Still they stood apart, not touching.

William's voice was hoarse. "Are you…all right?"

She nodded, and choked out, "Billy, he—he's got my daughter. My Emma."

William's hard gaze shot to Mac, who was taking in this little reunion with interest. "I warned you—"

"I knew it. You two *do* know each other—from the old Hollywood days, am I right?" Mac's grin was malignant. "Chill out, *Billy*. Emma's not hurt. I caught her snooping around. What was I supposed to do, let her get the cops on my tail?"

"She leaves with her mother. Bring her here."

"No one goes anywhere until I get paid. I've waited too damn long already."

The angry voices faded as Logan skulked around to the rear of the house, picking his way in the dark until he reached the basement window, set behind a brick-lined window well. Squatting on the bricks, bracing one hand against the wall, he snapped the top louvered pane with a sharp tap of his heel. He plucked the two halves of glass from their frame before they could clatter into the rock-lined well, then dispatched the remaining panes the same way, swiftly and noiselessly.

No sound came from behind the plywood covering the opening. His senses were on the alert; anything could be behind that barrier. Drawing his nine-millimeter, he let fly with a solid kick. The plywood groaned and cracked, leaking spears of light from the room below. One more well-placed blow splintered the board—and a good portion of the paneling it was nailed to.

Weapon at the ready, he peered down into the room and saw Emma Sutcliffe tied hand and foot to a straight chair—exactly the way he'd left her sister, except he hadn't shoved a grubby cloth in Zara's mouth. Emma was staring up at him, her eyes huge.

It seemed his brother had come to the same conclusion he had: trussing her up was the only way to get a Sutcliffe woman to stay put.

"It's Logan," he whispered, and she nodded vigorously, obviously realizing Mac would have no reason to break into his own basement. His limited interactions with Emma before Gage had taken her to Arkansas had shown her to be resourceful and level-headed. He hoped those qualities remained in good supply after her recent ordeal—she might need them tonight.

He eased himself through the window opening, feetfirst. It was a tight fit. Shards of wood snagged his jeans and windbreaker and gouged a furrow in his cheek. He dropped lightly to the worn tile floor, crossed to Emma and pulled the rag out of her mouth.

"He took Mom upstairs," she whispered urgently as he sliced her bindings with his penknife. "He's never done that—"

"Shh, I know. It's all right." He crept up the wooden steps toward the closed door, alert for sounds of Mac returning for Emma.

"Is Zara all right? I've been so—"

"She's fine. She's, uh—" *tied up at the moment* "—here in town, somewhere safe."

She started to follow him, but he waved her back. "Stay here!"

"I heard voices. Someone else is up there."

"It's someone named William—he's trying to buy your mother's release," he whispered. "She called him Billy."

She gasped. "Oh, my God. Mom was right. It *was* Billy! Logan, he's—"

"Shh!" He tested the doorknob—yes! Mac had left it unlocked, obviously figuring Emma wasn't going anywhere. "Stay down here!" he repeated.

He let himself out and moved through the first floor, silent as a wraith, following the sound of voices. Passing through the kitchen into the dining room, he slipped around the perimeter and hugged the wall next to the arched entrance into the living room.

Logan hoped Mac would acquiesce to William's demand and head back downstairs to fetch Emma. With his brother safely isolated from the others, Logan could surprise him, subdue him, and no civilian would get hurt in the process.

And then it would be over. His tormented brother would get the help he needed, and Logan would have peace. He'd be able to get on with his life. And so would his victims.

William was saying, "I don't think you fully appreciate how precarious your situation is, Mac. You've gotten sloppy, allowed your greed to affect your judgment."

"Don't give me that crap. We have a deal."

"Do we? Try this deal on for size. I walk out of here with Candy and Emma. In return, I refrain from turning you in to the authorities."

Mac sneered, "While we're on the subject of precarious situations—how far do you think an old gimp like you would make it to the door?"

"You're assuming no one knows I'm here."

In the strained silence that followed, Logan could almost smell his brother's escalating panic. He tightened his grip on his weapon. Mac was unpredictable under the best of circumstances.

Mac growled, "You're bluffing. The last thing a guy in your position would do is let it leak that he's tangled up in nasty business like this."

"Oh, my sensibilities aren't quite so delicate as all that, Mac. I've survived worse—and from men who make you look like an Eagle Scout. This isn't a battle you're going to win."

Logan tensed at Candy's shrill cry. Mac must have grabbed her. The fearful whimper that followed told him her life was in immediate peril—Mac was armed.

William's voice was tight, controlled. "Hurting Candy can gain you nothing."

"Call off your watchdogs, then we'll talk."

Logan heard Emma racing up the basement stairs, obviously alarmed by her mother's scream. In the heartbeat of time it took his trained mind to analyze the situation—and the inherent potential for disaster—Logan had already swung into the archway, gun leveled at his brother.

Startled, Mac jerked around to face him, using Candy as a shield, a small semiautomatic pressed to her temple. If Logan had harbored any lingering hope that his brother was sane, it shriveled as he stared into those hard golden eyes so like his own. And yet so alien.

William and Candy appeared momentarily stunned at seeing their nemesis confronted by a virtual clone of himself. Emma charged into the dining room. Without breaking eye contact with Mac, he waved her behind him.

William stood tense and watchful, obviously frustrated by the limitations of his damaged body. Candy's eyes were fixed on Logan; she appeared frightened but alert. Instinct told him he could count on her not to panic and make some sudden wrong move.

Mac said, "Have you folks met my illustrious brother? The hotshot G-man. Or I should say *former* G-man." He chuckled. "Even the damn FBI was too corrupt for him!"

"Don't make this worse, Mac. I know you want to end this thing as much as I do."

Logan's two-handed grip on his gun never wavered. Only *he* was aware of the tension radiating into his arms, his hands, his finger poised on the trigger.

Don't take aim if you're not prepared to shoot. It was the first thing the firearms instructor had taught him at the academy.

Was he prepared to look into his brother's eyes, his *own* eyes, and pull the trigger?

He felt sweat pop out on his upper lip. His eyes burned, staring without blinking, staring at this brother whom he both loved and hated. Could he? If he got a clear shot...?

Mac's eyes glowed with triumph. "You can't do

it, can you, bro? You can't shoot *me*. Hey, remember
when I broke into the Tarantinos' garage and swiped
those bikes? Remember how you stood up for me,
backed up my alibi? What were we then, twelve, thir-
teen? Forty bucks, I got for those bikes. We laughed
like hell after and split a pizza. A whole pizza, remember? 'Cause I had all that cash burning a hole in
my pocket.''

He addressed his captive audience. ''That's the
kind of brother this guy is. Loyal. Remember those
days, bro?''

Logan remembered. He didn't want to, but the
memories swarmed in on him from all directions. The
fights. The laughs. The scrapes with the law. The way
the two of them always stuck together. The deep love
he felt for this brother whom he'd always tried to
protect.

He thought of his mother's tear-choked plea before
he drove away that morning. *Whatever he's done, Logan, he's still family.*

Candy's dark eyes remained glued to Logan's. He
read fear, yes, but more than that, trust. In him. This
woman was counting on him to save her life.

It was no more than he'd promised her daughter—
his passionate, tormented, hardheaded Zara, who'd
managed in six short days to peel away years' worth
of cynicism and mistrust and expose a man he'd
thought long gone.

Trust me, he'd told her. *I'll do everything in my
power to end this, to see your mother and your sister
safe.*

His grip eased and his mind cleared. Infused with

a renewed sense of purpose, a cold resolve, he steadied his aim.

Mac said, "You know you're not going to shoot me, Logan. Toss the gun over here."

Logan doubted his brother's sophomoric fixation on Candy Carmelle would do her any good now. At that moment Mac's actions were driven by panic, and by his hatred for Logan.

When Logan failed to obey, Mac jerked Candy tighter and adjusted the angle of the gun barrel against her temple. Behind him, Emma gasped softly. William tensed, his knuckles gleaming white around the brass handle of the cane.

Mac said, "If you don't lose the gun within the next five seconds, she's dead."

Logan knew he wasn't bluffing. He tossed his nine-millimeter at his brother's feet. Grinning, Mac knelt with Candy, grabbed the gun and pocketed it, then started backing up to the front door, hauling his hostage along with him.

What would he do with her when he got away? The answer was obvious. She was of no further use to him. Logan's backup weapon, a slim .380, was holstered under his jeans at the small of his back. He prayed Mac would become overconfident and lower his guard. But just as in the old days, his brother seemed to read his mind.

"Keep those hands high, bro. Don't make me nervous." Mac reached the door and groped behind him for the knob. Holding Candy in a viselike grip, he eased the door open and started to back through...

And froze when his head encountered the muzzle of a gun.

Zara materialized behind him, holding the .357 Magnum Logan had left with Mrs. Feeney.

The *unloaded* .357 Magnum!

Emma whimpered, "Zara. Oh, God."

Zara said, "Give me the gun, Mac."

His obdurate expression told Logan he had no intention of cooperating. Zara thumbed the hammer back. Moonlight glinted on the cylinder as it revolved with a well-oiled *snap-clunk*. Mac flinched.

"Do it," she said.

Did she know there were no bullets in that thing? If so, she was gambling for high stakes—her own life and her mother's. Her audacity and courage humbled him. How had he ever imagined this woman as selfish and spoiled?

"All right..." Mac held the gun up, and Zara took it from him. Candy ran to Emma as Logan drew the .380, all too aware that Mac was still armed.

"Hands behind your head!" he barked, advancing on him.

Mac started to obey even as his eyes flicked to Zara standing in the doorway, blocking his escape route.

Logan shouted, *"No!"*

Mac spun toward Zara, pulling Logan's nine-millimeter from his pocket and training it on her in one smooth motion.

The .380 erupted in Logan's hands. Mac jerked but remained on his feet. Staring at his brother in wonder, he touched the small red stain on his chest.

The enormity of what he'd done slammed into Logan with sickening force. He watched Mac's dazed expression turn venomous, watched as he began raising his weapon one last time, taking aim at his brother.

Logan's initial shot had been an automatic response, an act of necessity to save Zara's life. Could he do it again, with cold calculation, staring directly into Mac's eyes? He steeled himself, knowing he had no choice.

Suddenly William was there, his arm arcing in a blur of motion. A resounding *crack!* sounded and Mac dropped heavily to the carpet, his legs crumpling under a savage blow from the older man's cane.

Logan's gun hand slowly dropped to his side, the .380 as heavy as a lead brick. Through a haze he heard movement, shaky voices, someone saying to call 911.

Vaguely he sensed Zara by his side, murmuring words of comfort in his ear, touching his face with cool, trembling fingers, urging him to turn away from the sight of his brother lying in a twisted heap, his lifeblood soaking into the carpet.

But he couldn't move. Couldn't respond. All he could do was stare into Mac's golden eyes, wide open but unseeing.

God forgive me.

Chapter Fourteen

Zara sat slumped on the plush burgundy sofa near the cold stone fireplace in Mac's den, staring at the high, wood-beamed ceiling. Emma and her mother sat on either side of her, and she held tightly to their hands, trying to ignore the bustle of activity in the living room.

The local police, a few uniforms and two plain-clothes detectives, had been joined by someone from the FBI. The coroner had arrived and was doing whatever grisly thing coroners do to dead bodies at a crime scene. Zara and the others had already been questioned separately. Candy and Emma were waiting to be taken to the local hospital for a checkup.

Logan was in the living room with the cops, filling them in on the details, as cool and in control as that first day when he'd grabbed her at Kennedy Airport. That could have been six months ago, rather than six days. She wasn't the same person she'd been then.

He'd zoned out for a while after the shooting. Nothing she said or did seemed to get through to him. He must have been in a kind of shock. It was understandable, after the horror he'd just been through—watching his brother die by his own hand.

But as soon as the authorities began arriving, he'd transformed into the consummate law enforcement type: cooperative, informative and frighteningly detached.

He'd ignored her, had politely rebuffed her efforts to get him alone or have any personal communication at all. No mention of what would happen in the future, or even the next hour.

Logan Byrne, her anchor, had cut her free. She felt helplessly adrift at a time when she needed him more than ever. And she was certain he needed her.

Billy Sharke, her mother's onetime movie director, sat opposite the women on a matching love seat. It was he who'd set this whole mess in motion by hiring Mac to procure the gun for his private collection. At the time, he'd believed, as had she, that Logan's brother was a legitimate dealer in art and collectibles.

She couldn't blame Billy for what had happened, and she no longer blamed herself—though that was one of her specialties, she now knew, taking the blame for others' failings. Mac Byrne alone was responsible for the horror she and her family had endured.

Emma leaned forward, looking past Zara to catch Candy's eye. "It's time."

Time for what? Zara wondered distractedly. Had she missed something?

She turned her head and looked at Candy. The sudden apprehension in her mother's expression alarmed her. She sat up straight. "Mom? What is it?"

Emma asked Candy, "Would you like me to tell—"

"No." Candy squeezed Zara's hand harder. "It's something I should've done long ago."

Affection infused Billy's baritone voice. "Candy…whatever you have to say, just give it to us straight, sweetheart. After what we've all been through, I don't think anything could come as a surprise."

"Oh…I don't know about that.…"

Zara was instantly on the alert. She'd never heard her mother sound timid before.

Candy looked Billy in the eye. "I never should have married John. It was the biggest mistake of my life."

He smiled wryly. "What a shocker. I kind of figured that one out for myself when your bridegroom crippled me and threatened both our lives."

Zara's heart slammed into her throat. *"What?"*

Billy looked contrite. "I'm sorry, I didn't realize—"

"It's all right," Candy said. "It's past time all this came to light. But the thing you never knew, Billy… It wasn't just you and me that were in danger. John said if I ever got in touch with you again, he'd…" She cast her anguished glance at Zara and Emma, her voice a hoarse whisper. "My babies…"

Billy paled. He leaned forward. "That animal threatened his own children?"

Zara covered her mother's trembling hand with both of hers. As shocking as these revelations were, she didn't doubt they were true.

Candy squeezed her eyes shut for a moment.

"They...the girls weren't his. He wasn't their father. And he knew that."

Billy's face reflected Zara's own dawning comprehension.

Candy said, "Emma and Zara are your daughters, Billy."

Billy slowly sat back. He stared at the twins, and they at him. Now that it had been said, the physical resemblance was unmistakable. The eyes. The mouth.

No one spoke. The truth trickled into Zara's consciousness like water in sand, filling the empty spaces in her soul. Completing her.

She'd never had a father before this day. That knowledge was somehow uplifting. She had a fresh start on being a daughter, on forging that special relationship.

Billy looked as if he'd been walloped with a two-by-four. "Daughters. I have two daughters."

Candy said, "I don't expect you to forgive me, Billy. I never stopped loving you, but I...I thought I could have something with John that you couldn't offer—something I'd dreamed of all my life. Respectability. A place in society. No more money worries. He seemed so devoted, so loving. At first."

She grimaced. "He could really turn on the charm when he wanted to. What I didn't realize then was that I was an ornament to him, nothing more. It was your basic whirlwind courtship. We were engaged before I knew I was pregnant. You were...well, you weren't exactly 'Father Knows Best' material back then. The crazy Hollywood life-style...and never enough money. When I found out I was expecting, I did what I thought was best for my baby—I went ahead and married John. I'm sorry, Billy. God, I'm so sorry."

Zara held her mother as she wept.

After a few moments Billy said quietly, "Candy...don't. Don't do this to yourself, sweetheart."

"But it was so wrong of me."

He sighed, and in that sound Zara heard weariness, compassion and regret for all that could never be. He said, "And if it had worked out the way you'd expected, if Sutcliffe had been a devoted husband and father, then what you did might not seem so wrong. We make decisions. Some of them, we wish we hadn't. God knows I have a few regrets of my own."

Candy looked up, her eyes red-rimmed. "I can't believe you're not angry. Thirty years ago you'd have thrown a fit if you'd found out what I'd done."

He smiled grimly. "Don't kid yourself. Thirty years ago I'd have torn the place apart. People change, Candy. The thing I don't get, though—I can't see a guy like Sutcliffe, all ego, raising someone else's kids as his own."

Candy said, "But that's what it was all about, don't you see? Ego. If he'd let it be known the girls weren't his, it would be like admitting to the world that his wife had gotten something over on him. Taking the girls from me was his way of punishing me."

Until that moment, Zara had never realized how alike Sutcliffe and her ex-husband were. Both had been unspeakably cruel to people they'd sworn to love and protect, all for the sake of their precious egos. Logan had been right about the twisted motives that drove them.

Emma said, "Billy—" She smiled self-consciously. "I don't know what to call you."

His answering smile was soft and downright paternal. "Billy's fine. But if you want to try 'Dad' on for size, I'm game."

She continued, "Mom said my fa—I mean, John Sutcliffe destroyed you. He had you discredited, blacklisted in Hollywood. You've obviously done very well for yourself despite all that."

"Have you ever heard of Magic in Motion?"

Zara answered. "It's one of the companies filmmakers hire to create special effects in their movies. Monsters, tornadoes, spaceships, whatever. M and M has been involved in a couple of my clients' pictures. Are you with the company?"

"I *am* the company. I created it."

Zara frowned. "But Roger Stevenson—"

"Roger's been with me from the beginning. He's the ostensible CEO, the front guy, and I'm—" he made a vaporous motion with his fingers "—invisible."

Emma's eyes shone with admiration. "You figured out a way to get around the blacklisting."

"In a way, Sutcliffe did me a favor. I was an okay director, but let's face it—no Spielberg. Back then, we had no budget to speak of on those cheap horror flicks. I had to roll up my sleeves and help hammer out the special effects—not that they were all that special. Giant rubber sea creatures and sheet-metal robots. But, God, I had a blast making them. When Sutcliffe destroyed my directing career, it seemed natural to switch gears and do what I really loved."

Candy smiled in fond remembrance. "Well, those

silly effects were special to *me*. I loved those giant rubber sea creatures and sheet-metal robots.''

He said, ''Don't forget the decapitated head with all the electrodes. That one's a work of art.''

Zara said, ''The thing under glass? Scowling like this?'' She screwed up her face.

''You've seen it?''

''Seen it! The disgusting thing's taking up space in my living room!''

''I should've known she'd make off with that piece, too. She got all my best stuff.'' He grinned proudly. ''Like a damn pack rat, your mother was.''

Zara snorted. ''Was?''

Candy said, ''They helped me feel closer to you, all those props. Your masterpieces.''

Emma asked, ''Did you construct the ray gun, too?''

''Of course. After filming, your mother had to have that ridiculous thing. She, uh, convinced me to give it to her, for her personal collection.''

Zara was beginning to figure it out. ''When you offered Mac Byrne two million dollars to buy it back from Mom, anonymously, you assumed he'd make a reasonable profit and that she'd get to keep most of that money. That was your way of trying to take care of her, wasn't it, Bil—Dad?''

He looked uncomfortable. He addressed Candy. ''I knew you'd been on your own most of those thirty years, and it hadn't been easy for you. I was sort of…keeping tabs. After Sutcliffe died five years ago and you still didn't try to get in touch, I figured you didn't want to hear from me.''

''I thought you'd hate me.''

"I could never hate you, sweetheart. The thing is, I...I've got a lot of money. More than I can spend. I didn't see why you shouldn't be comfortable."

Candy held his gaze, misty-eyed and wobbly-chinned. At last her face crumpled on a hiccuping sob.

"Oh, Lord..." Billy heaved himself off the love seat. "Sweetheart, I can't stand to see you like this."

She gulped, "I—I—I—I—"

He made his way to her and lifted her to her feet. She bawled, "I don't deserve you! I never did."

He wrapped her in his arms. "Agreed. What do you say I let you spend the *next* thirty years making it up to me?"

Zara bit her lip on a smile. It sounded like something Logan would say. The idea of her mother spending the rest of her life with Billy Sharke—her father!—warmed her right down to her toes.

He looked at Zara and her sister over their mother's head. His eyes glistened. "We all have a lot of catching up to do. I just want you to know...I'm proud as hell to be your old man."

Zara laughed and blinked back her own tears. "Hate to break the news to you. I don't go around disarming bad guys every day."

"We're even," he said. "I don't go around knee-capping 'em with my cane, either." He kissed Candy's platinum head.

Detective Jackson poked his head in. "Your ride's here, ladies."

Zara rose with them. "I'll go with you. I just want a word with Logan first."

The detective said, "Oh, he already left, Miss Sutcliffe."

Her heart constricted. "Where did he go?" She regretted the stupid question the instant it left her mouth.

Detective Jackson shrugged. "Not to Tahiti, that's all I know. I asked him to stick close to home for a while, till we get this whole thing straightened out. Same goes for all of you."

Stick close to home. She should have been thrilled at the prospect. Her apartment. The agency. Her old routine. Her smooth clean sheets and her cappuccino maker and her drawer full of naughty undies that she used to wear just for herself, wondering what all the fuss was about.

She wished she'd never found out.

Chapter Fifteen

Zara unlocked the steel door next to the closed warehouse bay, grateful that she still had the key she'd wangled from Logan.

She hadn't heard word one from him these last two and a half weeks since Mac's death. He hadn't answered his phone or returned the messages she'd left on his machine. She'd even gone to his apartment on Manhattan's West Side in the area once known as Hell's Kitchen—not too far from the warehouse, as it turned out. He was home, she was certain, but he didn't answer her persistent knocking. She'd vowed then and there to wash her hands of the man. He obviously didn't want anything to do with her.

Yet here she was, still tracking him down, tenacious as a bloodhound. Those six days she'd spent with him were burned into her soul, taking up much more psychic space than they had a right to. When she'd left him standing over Mac's body, talking to the detectives, she couldn't have guessed that would be her last glimpse of him. He'd never even said, "So long, it's been real."

She knew that anguish and guilt had caused him to

withdraw from her, and from everyone else. He'd been forced to do the unspeakable—to take his own brother's life. She empathized with the hell he had to be going through. But he didn't have to go through it alone.

He'd taught her to trust. It was high time she returned the favor.

He'd go where he feels safe, Lou had told her. *Some secluded place where he can lick his wounds in private.* She knew of only one place that fit the bill.

Every sound seemed magnified in the deserted building—the clang of the heavy door slamming shut behind her, the clicking of high heels on concrete. There were no windows here on the first floor, just unrelieved gray-painted cinder-block walls and concrete-sheathed columns standing sentry at regular intervals. The overhead fluorescent light fixtures had been left on—a clue that her quarry might indeed be in residence.

She click-clicked across the floor to the freight elevator and pushed the call button. A deep mechanical rumble heralded its arrival. Through the thick, wired-glass window she watched it descend. The wide doors opened vertically, parting up and down instead of sideways.

Stooping, she pulled the steel-slat safety gate up, stepped inside the enormous elevator and closed the gate. She pushed five, followed by Close. And rode the grinding, clanking contraption up five flights, staring at the scraped-up embossed steel floor and graffiti-covered walls she'd hoped never to see again.

The things one did for love.

Was that what this was? She'd always thought love

was supposed to hit you like a rubber mallet—and leave you floating on a cloud. What she felt was much more complex, and in some ways, much more prosaic.

Frustration.

Exasperation.

Worry.

With just a dollop of compassion to keep her off balance.

On the fifth floor she inserted her key in the lock and pushed open the door to her onetime safe house. Clouds of dust motes drifted in the shafts of late morning light streaming in through the filthy windows.

Her eyes zeroed in on that putrid old mattress, now littered with empty coffee cups, deli bags and assorted sections of the Sunday *Times*. Logan sat in the middle of the mess, nine-millimeter in hand, aimed at her heart.

Zara raised her hands. "Don't shoot. I've got a check for you from Publishers Clearing House."

He let the gun dangle over his raised knee. He didn't speak, but he didn't have to. His eyes were brutally eloquent. *What the hell are you doing here?*

She started toward him. "Need help with the crossword?" A memory came to her of another Sunday morning when the two of them had lolled around on this mattress together, trying to think of a seven-letter word for "afflicted," starting with *s*. The answer only came to her yesterday.

Smitten.

He set the gun aside and held out his hand, palm up.

Fat chance. Smiling sweetly, she opened her small black patent shoulder bag and ostentatiously dropped the warehouse key inside. She clicked the bag shut.

She paused at the edge of the mattress, hands on hips, staring down at him. From his vantage point he probably had a sensational view up her short, body-hugging electric blue dress. Good.

He was barefoot and shirtless this warm June morning, dressed only in jeans. His long hair was loose, due more to indifference, she suspected, than choice. A couple of days' worth of whiskers studded his strong jaw. He looked uncivilized. Virile.

Irresistible.

"You look like hell," she said.

"Go." He licked his fingertip and turned to the op-ed page.

"I don't think so. We need to talk."

"*I* need to be alone to read the damn paper. If *you* need to talk, I suggest you find someone who wants to listen."

"Logan—"

Before she even registered movement, he'd reached up and yanked her shoulder bag. She tried to hold on to it and ended up sprawled on her belly atop the Arts and Leisure section. Pinning her with a knee to her back, he opened the purse and upended it over her fanny. The contents rolled off her and scattered. She jerked when his fingers plunged between her thighs, groping from her knees to the hiked-up hem of her stretchy dress. If this was his idea of foreplay...

He withdrew his hand, flipped her over and displayed his prize—the key. He slipped it into his jeans pocket.

"Now." He pulled her to a sitting position and shoved her empty purse at her. "Go away or I'll toss your butt on the street. I don't want you here. I can't make it any plainer than that."

"Ah, still the same silver-tongued rascal. You don't mind if I collect my things, do you?" She lifted her wallet and took her time tucking it into a corner of the purse, just so.

He sighed heavily, watching her scan the mattress for the next logical item to pack. "How the hell did you get all that stuff in that little bitty bag anyway?"

He'd advanced from threats to nonsensical questions. She supposed that was progress.

"Watch and learn from the master," she answered, lifting a corner of the newspaper, searching for her checkbook. "The key is to pack each item in the correct order, and in the precise spot where it belongs."

He regarded her in stony silence, sitting cross-legged with his arms folded over his chest, imperious as a pasha. Finally he blurted, "Okay. How'd you get away from Baby Jane?"

She smiled. That question must have been driving him crazy for two and a half weeks. "I calmly suggested she call the FBI and ask them if there's an agent named Logan Pierce."

"And she did it?"

"She pretended to ignore me at first, but I could tell I'd gotten her thinking. She started knitting faster and faster, making all these mistakes. Finally she picked up the phone."

"Keep packing."

She looked around at the jumble of her belongings.

"Now, where is that lipstick?" Under her butt, if she wasn't mistaken.

He asked, "Did you know the revolver was unloaded?"

"I figured it out. Played with it till that round thing swung open that holds the bullets...?"

"The cylinder."

"I looked in all the little spaces and they were empty. And there was no ammo in your duffel—you must've taken it out."

"Did you really think I was going to leave Baby Jane with bullets?"

"I suppose I should be thankful for small favors."

He raked his fingers through his hair. "Zara, you could've gotten yourself killed, pulling a stunt like that—confronting Mac with an unloaded weapon."

"He had my mother, Logan. I saw everything through the window. Besides, I figured I had surprise on my side."

He just stared at her, and what she read in his expression just then made up for nineteen days of silence. Almost.

He said, "I couldn't have asked for better backup. You did a hell of a job."

"We make a good team."

The light faded from his eyes and he looked away. "I mean it, Zara. I need to be alone."

"Why? So you can keep beating yourself up over what you were forced to do?"

"No one forced me to do anything. I had a choice."

"You're right. You could've chosen to let your brother kill me."

"I could've wounded him. Shot him in the arm, the shoulder..."

"Is that what they taught you at the academy? To take careful aim at a gunman's shoulder when he's about to shoot an innocent victim? You acted quickly, automatically, the way you were no doubt trained. It's not like you made this decision, I'm going to kill my brother now."

He sighed. "Zara, I don't expect you to understand."

"You're right. No one else can really understand what you're going through. I can try, though. I know I hurt for you. I hurt so badly for you, Logan." Her voice cracked.

"All my life I tried to protect my brother, to take care of him. So did my folks, in their way."

"How are they taking it?"

He was silent awhile. "Better than I'd expected. I think, in a way, they knew it was inevitable."

She said softly, "I think you did, too."

His gaze turned inward. "I keep replaying it in my mind. Those last few seconds."

"Did you expect him to just give up and surrender quietly?"

He was about to lie and say yes, she could tell. Instead he shook his head. She wanted to touch him, to comfort him, but she sensed he wasn't ready for that.

She said, "I'll tell you how it looked from where I was standing. Mac knew it was over, knew he couldn't get away. You were standing right there, holding a gun on him. And he knew that *you* knew he had that second gun in his pocket—yours."

"What's your point?"

"He knew you were watching him like a hawk, in case he made a move for that gun." She let that hang there.

"And he did. So what?"

"So it was his choice, don't you see? He took the decision out of your hands. He could've cooperated, let you disarm him. He could have let himself be taken into custody and eventually ended up in a mental facility, like you wanted. But he chose to pull that gun, forcing you to stop him. He knew he didn't have a prayer of getting away."

"Are you saying he had a death wish?"

"No. Not really. I just think he wanted the horror to end as badly as you did. He was tormented, fanatically jealous of you. That night he tried to drown me, he slipped so easily into pretending he was you."

Logan looked pensive. "And he used my name for his alias in Hobart."

"But he could never become you. It was like some...violation of the natural order, the two of you coexisting. Two incompatible halves of one whole."

"Seems I'm not the only one who's given this some thought."

She was pleased that she'd managed to get through to him, at least a little. "I would've liked to talk to you about all this back then."

He hesitated. "There was no point. It's over."

Her chest squeezed painfully. *What's over?* she wanted to ask. The terrible ordeal...or the beauty that came out of it, what the two of them shared?

He continued, "I saw no sense in prolonging things, Zara."

She tried to smile, but bitterness infused her voice. "Is this what they call a clean break?"

"It's for the best."

"I...I can understand if being with me reminds you of...what happened. Maybe it feels to you like our relationship is...I don't know, tainted in some way. We can talk about it, Logan, we can work around it." She despised the pleading tone in her voice. Where had this desperation come from? When had he become as important to her as the air she breathed?

His expression hardened in exasperation. "It's not that. You're making this harder than it has to be. I thought I made it clear back then that there's no future for us."

There it was. He didn't want her. He'd tried to let her down the kindest way he knew how—by ending it abruptly. Her eyes stung with tears of humiliation.

She started grabbing her scattered belongings and shoving them into her purse helter-skelter. She couldn't bear to look at him, afraid of what she'd see in his eyes. The disdain. Or, worse, pity.

She whipped the newspapers aside and grabbed her tissues, compact and comb, shoving them into her purse as she staggered to her feet.

"Uh...you missed something," he said. She turned back and saw the small box that had tumbled over the side of the mattress. *Ribbed for her pleasure.*

Her mortification was now complete. She snatched up the box and crammed it into the overstuffed bag, her face hot as a griddle. She sprinted toward the door as quickly as her heels would allow.

"Zara. Don't..."

Don't go away mad, just go away. Wasn't that how it went?

He swore softly. "You're taking this the wrong way."

Yanking the door open, she almost laughed, but it would have ended in tears. Exactly how many ways were there to take it?

She stabbed the elevator call button and waited impatiently. Once inside, she pressed the ground-floor button and Close. As the doors started closing she heard the warehouse door open and Logan's voice bellowing at her to wait up. She jabbed the G button again, hard, as if that would get her there faster. Her fingernail snapped.

She jumped as a resounding blow shook the closed doors. Logan's fist, no doubt. The elevator started its creaky descent.

She wished she'd never sought him out. How foolish of her to assume he shared her feelings. What had been wondrous and unique to her had been simply a passing diversion to him. One of many, no doubt.

On the ground floor the doors slid open. She yelped in alarm when the safety gate rolled up before she could touch it. Logan must have sprinted down the five flights of stairs, though he didn't appear the least bit winded. She tried to scoot past him, but he looped a long arm around her waist, hauled her back inside the elevator, closed the gate and punched the Close button for good measure.

The harsh light from above picked out sharp angles in his face, turned it into a menacing landscape of light and shadow. "You are going to listen to me."

"I listened. You made yourself perfectly clear."

"I don't think I did."

"You want me to make this easy for you!" she cried. "You want me to tell you it's okay for you to do this to me—to make me care and then walk away. It's not okay!"

After a moment he said quietly, "I never meant to do that. God knows I never wanted to hurt you, Zara."

There it was. Pity. He was leaving her with nothing, not even the shreds of her pride. "What do you want me to say?" she asked wearily. "Is your conscience bothering you, is that it? All right, then. It was a simple misunderstanding and not your fault at all. You never meant to lead me on, but silly Zara, starved for love, took the whole thing much too seriously."

"Zara—"

"As a casual sexual partner, you were a paragon of consideration. You didn't pressure me, you saw to my gratification. Why, you even used a condom without being asked!"

"Zara, stop this."

"Is that what you wanted to hear? Can I go now?"

He braced one palm on a graffiti-covered wall and dropped his head a moment, as if seeking divine guidance. "I tried to make you understand, back when we..." He sighed, and when he looked up, she saw all her own heartache reflected in his eyes. He said softly, "I can't give you what you need...what you deserve. I don't have it in me. I'll only cause you more pain."

"I don't believe that," she whispered.

He smiled sadly. "You don't know me that well."

"Famous last words. Isn't that what I once told you? That you didn't know me like Tony did? I was wrong. You saw right through my insecurities, my hurts. You made me open up to you, made me look at myself in a way I never had before. You made me believe in myself—and in you."

He said nothing.

"You made me *need* you, dammit!" After a strained silence she said, "I just want one thing and you'll never hear from me again. I want to hear you say you don't feel anything for me."

"That's not what this is about."

"What else is there! That's the *only* thing it's about, Logan. It's why you paid that little visit to Tony last week."

He frowned. "How did you find out about that?"

"Mutual acquaintances."

"It was just something that had to be done, that's all," he said gruffly. "The bastard needed an attitude adjustment."

Along with nose, tooth and rib adjustments, if her sources were correct. "Well, I may be old-fashioned," she said, "but I always thought fighting for a woman's honor indicated a certain level of commitment."

"I care, Zara, I'm not going to deny it. But it's not enough by itself. This commitment you're talking about is built on more than just feelings. The last few years have changed me. I'm not the man I used to be."

"But maybe you're a better man now. Did you think of that? Painful experiences harden us, but they also bring forth strengths and inner resources we didn't know we had. Just ask John Sutcliffe," she added wryly. "I don't think he expected his aggressive child-rearing techniques to stir up all that mutinous self-reliance. Maybe your sensitivity is the result of whatever horrible things *you've* had to deal with."

"Sensitivity!" He couldn't have looked more astonished if she'd accused him of cross-dressing.

"You don't think you're sensitive? What about when you asked me if Tony ever gave me encouragement, a shoulder to cry on? If he supported me emotionally? Logan, you opened my eyes to what a relationship is supposed to be. You seem to have a better handle on it all than I do."

"Hell, that stuff's just common sense."

She smiled. "Believe it or not, that sort of sense isn't as common as you might believe. Face it, big guy. You're sensitive."

He didn't look amused.

"Don't worry," she said. "I won't tell anyone."

"This isn't going to work," he muttered, but the words lacked conviction. "I've told you before, Zara. There's a piece of me that's just not there."

She closed the short distance to take his hand in hers. "That's because you've already given it to me. Straight from your heart to mine." She placed his palm between her breasts. "Before you, I wasn't whole. That's the way you put it, and you were right. I've changed, healed—*you've* done that for me. You've given me that piece of yourself and completed me."

Logan shook his head with a little smile of admiration. "Must be hell trying to negotiate a deal with you. I'll bet those publishers and movie people scatter when they see you coming.''

"They run like cheap panty hose.''

He ran his hands over her hips, pulling her closer. "Now, how would you know about panty hose, cheap or otherwise?''

His fingers slipped under her short hem and traced the edges of her sheer black stockings. A delicious shiver raced through her. He lowered his head and kissed her the way she'd imagined being kissed these last two and a half weeks. Through the voluptuous haze she felt him reach behind her with both hands. After a few seconds of fumbling, one garter hook popped open.

Breathless, she broke the kiss. "What are you doing?''

"Don't have my knife on me.'' He released the other back hook and started working on the front ones.

She looked around at the huge, grimy freight elevator. "Here?''

"Unless you'd prefer that lovely mattress upstairs.''

"No! Here is just fine.''

He pulled her royal blue silk panties down her hips and eased them over her high heels. He looped them on one of the steel buttons studding the wall near the ceiling, usually used to support heavy protective padding.

"See?'' he said. "All the conveniences.''

She couldn't have cared less about conveniences. She'd make love with this man anywhere, anytime. All he had to do was touch her—Lord, just *look* at her in that certain way—and a lifetime of propriety took wing.

He said, "My knife's not the only thing I don't have on me. Good thing you came prepared."

He rummaged in the gaping purse still hanging on her shoulder and produced the box of condoms. He plucked out one square packet, pocketed it and dropped the rest. The purse slid to the embossed metal floor, disgorging its contents for the second time that morning. Her compact crashed in a spray of powder. Her lipstick rolled into the corner.

She barely noticed, enthralled by Logan's voracious kisses, his impatient hands, the leashed power in his hard, half-naked body. Her own hands and mouth roamed restlessly, frantic for the touch of him, the taste of him. She feasted her senses like a woman starved. A thumping hunger settled between her legs and she felt herself unfurl like a dew-drenched rose.

She tugged at his belt, yanking it from the buckle with a snap of leather. She struggled with the brass button of his jeans, until his hand slid under her dress. Then all she could do was grab him for support.

"Logan…please…" she whimpered in a frenzy of need. "Now!"

"Open it." He indicated his fly.

She forced her fingers to move, forced herself to concentrate on working his zipper. She tugged the jeans and briefs down, freeing him. And all the while he stroked her, probed her, touched her right *there,* until she was half out of her mind.

He handed her the packet. "You do it."

He might as well have asked her to pilot a 747; her wits had long since deserted her. He continued to caress her as she tore at the thing with shaking hands, finally ripping it open with her teeth. She knew he was tormenting her on purpose, enjoying her loss of control.

She chuckled. "I'll pay you back for this."

"I can hardly wait."

She tossed the torn packet and applied herself to the task of sheathing him, a new experience for her. He watched the process avidly, groaning as she smoothed the thin latex down his rigid penis. His own control was near the breaking point, too, she could tell, as he unceremoniously hiked up her snug dress.

"Hold on now." He lifted her by the hips, opening her legs and wrapping them around his waist. He never took his eyes from hers as he drove into her in one powerful thrust. They cried out in unison, a triumphant sound. She knew at that moment they were one not only in flesh but in spirit, as well. He throbbed deep inside her, and her body answered with involuntary little spasms.

He groaned, "I don't want it to end. I wish we could stay like this forever."

"Someone may need the elevator someday."

"Let 'em use the stairs." The muscles in his arms bunched as he lifted her, holding her empty and aching for a long heartbeat before lowering her on his length once more. He smiled at her shuddering gasp of fulfillment. His powerful arms moved her in a timeless rhythm, bringing her closer and closer to the searing brink of orgasm.

She clung tightly to his flexing shoulders, wondering how long a person could endure this degree of pleasure and stay sane. She was a wild thing, panting, riding him, blindly seeking his mouth with her own. Needing to be connected to him in every possible way.

And then her climax was nearly upon her, just out of reach but moving in swiftly, like a gathering storm. Sweet, sharp anticipation spiked ever higher with each hammering stroke, until it hit like a typhoon.

Logan succumbed to his release in the same charged instant. Together they rode it out, holding fast to each other, moving as one.

Afterward they remained wrapped around each other, all sweat-slick arms and legs, not a hairbreadth of space between them. Their hearts played bumper cars. Zara roused herself, lifted her head from his shoulder. His eyes were heavy-lidded, deliciously slumberous.

She mumbled, "Mmm...thirsty."

"All that panting and screaming will do that."

"Oh!" She tried to pummel his rump with her heel, but with little success. He tightened his hold, and his laughing eyes turned solemn.

"Zara, I do love you. I don't think I told you that."

Her heart swelled till she thought it would burst. "No." She laughed at the sudden tears that clogged her throat. "I don't think you did. I love you, too, Logan. I've never been in love before."

"That makes two of us. We'll just have to muddle through together."

"Hey, we make a hell of a team, remember? We'll get it figured out."

He gently set her down on her own wobbly legs and bent to retrieve the pack of tissues that had fallen out of her purse. A few moments later they were both decent, if rumpled. Logan squatted to help gather the contents of her purse.

"Oh, my God!" She touched the bite wound on his shoulder, ran her fingers over the claw marks. "Did *I* do this?"

He craned his head to look. "The price of being a world-class lover. There's always the risk of permanent bodily injury."

She smirked. "Remind me never to become a world-class lover."

"Too late. Didn't you notice those finger marks on your fanny?"

She rubbed her sore bottom through her dress. "No, but now that you mention it…"

"What can I say? You make me forget myself."

She picked up the box of condoms and tried to squeeze it into the overstressed bag. "Guess I should've brought a bigger purse."

"Oh, you won't be taking those home." He plucked the box from her fingers.

"I won't?"

His slow, suggestive grin said, *Trust me on this.* He punched the button for the fifth floor. The elevator jerked and started its grinding ascent.

She wrinkled her nose. "Logan, that mattress…"

"There's the desk, the chair, the coffee table. Have you ever done it on a windowsill?"

His words drew intriguing images in her mind. She asked, "Have *you* ever done it in an elevator before?"

"Nope."

"So what do you think?"

"It has its—" She slapped a hand over his mouth,

but he still managed a garbled, "Ups and downs." The elevator stopped and he raised the slatted gate.

She said, "I'm surprised at you, Logan. A sorry old gag like that from a world-class lover?"

"With enough inspiration, I'm sure I can come up with something more original." He held open the door to the warehouse and gestured grandly. "Inspire me."

Epilogue

Candy had never heard the wedding march played with quite this much enthusiasm—or improvisation. Trust Zara to choose a Dixieland band. Emma had held out for a sedate string quartet, but after Zara took her to hear some New Orleans-style jazz, she changed her mind. "Feel-good music," Emma had dubbed it. The decision was made.

About three hundred guests occupied the rows of chairs that had been set up on the enormous lawn of Zara and Logan's new home on Long Island—a wedding present from Billy. It was a perfect early autumn afternoon, mild and sunny.

The instant they heard the familiar tune, everyone turned toward the rear of the flower-bedecked aisle. Tears welled in Candy's eyes as she spotted her husband standing between their daughters, his arms linked with theirs. Billy Sharke still took her breath away every time she looked at him. He was more handsome than he'd been thirty years earlier when she'd first fallen in love with him.

He'd invited her to share in the honor of walking the twin brides down the aisle, but she'd declined.

For once in her life, tradition had won out. She wanted to enjoy the picture-perfect symmetry of her beautiful daughters sharing this momentous walk with their father.

Her family.

Emma was wearing her grandma Sarro's wedding dress, a high-necked column of ivory satin, seed pearls and delicate handmade lace. She looked sixteen with her long, dark hair worn straight and simple, her crown ringed by a circlet of ivory rosebuds from which fell an exquisite floor-length veil. Candy was happy her mother was there to see it. Beside her, she heard Mama's soft, awe-filled gasp.

Zara had chosen satin, too: the futuristic wedding dress from *Atomic Bride,* the costume that had been on display in her living room the last few months. The white satin concoction was very short, nipped in at the waist and flared at the hips. It boasted an enormous winglike collar that framed her face and accented the down-to-there neckline. A perky matching cap sat askew on her short hair. Thigh-high white satin boots with four-inch heels completed the look. Say what you will, it was a memorable outfit. Judy Jetson meets Madonna.

Billy's limp was barely noticeable during the leisurely processional. He glowed with pride, and the girls looked happier than she'd ever seen them. Logan's friend Louise gave Zara a thousand-watt smile as they passed. Her daughter, Holly, offered a thumbs-up to the outrageous outfit.

Billy escorted his daughters to their bridegrooms, flanking the minister. He kissed them, shook the men's hands, then joined Candy in the front row, but not before giving his mother-in-law's furrowed cheek a warm kiss.

He squeezed Candy's hand, and she fought to hold back tears of joy. If she started bawling now, she wasn't likely to stop. All the wedding photos would show her with red eyes and smeared mascara.

She still couldn't get over the fact that these two hunks were about to become her sons-in-law. Gage Foster was six feet plus of robust Dixie charm. Blue eyes. Thick light brown hair. He reminded her of Harrison Ford, ruggedly elegant in a charcoal suit and blue shirt, complete with string tie and cowboy boots.

And then there was Logan Byrne. Even though he was physically identical to the man who'd kidnapped and terrorized her, Candy never confused the two in her mind. Logan was the antithesis of his demented brother.

He looked painfully handsome in a navy blue double-breasted suit, white shirt and an exquisite silk tie in shades of red. His dark hair was pulled off his face in a ponytail, and he was smiling at his bride in a way that told Candy their wedding night would be one for the record books.

The minister began, "Friends, we're doubly blessed today, to witness and rejoice as not one, but two couples declare their love and commitment before God…"

Mama started sniffling at that point, as did Candy's seven sisters and sisters-in-law sitting behind her, and it was all she could do not to join them. She gave up the fight at the end of the moving service when her new sons-in-law kissed their brides with such fervor that the guests erupted in cheers and applause. The band struck up "Sweet Georgia Brown" as the beaming brides retraced their steps down the aisle on their husbands' arms.

The couples and their parents greeted each guest in turn in a reception line, after which waiters distributed flutes of champagne. Billy's deep, mellifluous voice got the crowd's attention.

"Four months ago, I thought I was the luckiest man alive to find myself the father of these two bright, talented, lovely young women. Today my joy is complete. Zara and Emma have found themselves men who can make them as happy as they deserve to be." He raised his glass. "After sixty-three years, I have a passel of in-laws, and it feels damn good!"

Everyone laughed and joined him in drinking to the newlyweds. Hors d'oeuvres and cocktails flowed as the hired help set out a sumptuous dinner buffet. The band was doing amazing things with "When the Saints Come Marching In." Guests mingled in clusters and around white-draped tables dotting the grounds. The photographer posed the couples for a few shots, then Candy and Billy with the brides, before setting off to corral the grooms' parents.

Candy noticed that Zara's and Emma's arms remained around each other's waists even after the photographer left. Over the past four months, she'd watched their relationship blossom. Crises had a way of straightening out one's priorities. She knew both of her daughters had vowed to put their strained past behind them and renew the close bond that should never have been allowed to lapse.

This double wedding was an auspicious beginning. Never would she have imagined these two opinionated young women capable of compromising on such profound issues as what brand of champagne to buy— Emma's Veuve Clicquot had won out—or whether the cake should be filled with raspberry preserves or ganache. Both found their way between the layers.

Billy said, "Gage, how's that new wing coming along?"

His wedding gift to Emma and Gage had been an extensive addition to Gage's sprawling log home tucked into the woods of rural Arkansas. Candy had visited them there and experienced the rustic opulence firsthand. Even a city girl like her had to admit it was a beautiful place to live, and to raise children.

Gage said, "It's nearly finished. Emma and I can't wait to move into the new office."

Zara said, "You two will be *sharing* an office? Good luck getting any work done."

Emma blushed. "Zara!"

"I thought true love had cured your priggish nature," Zara teased. "Guess I was wrong."

Despite Emma's knee-jerk reaction, Candy knew she had indeed loosened up a lot over the last few months, since Gage had come into her life. It had worked both ways. Emma's encouragement and support had helped him find self-respect and gratification in his new career, writing bestselling medical thrillers. An injury to his hand had forced the former surgeon out of the operating room, and the adjustment hadn't been easy.

"As a matter of fact," Emma said, "Gage and I work exceptionally well together. We brainstorm on each other's books. We're like a two-person critique group."

After moving to Arkansas with her fiancé, Emma had happily relinquished her brand-new, detested job as a staff writer at *Crafty Lady* magazine in New York. Her new home—or was it her new man?—had proven inspirational. Not only had she started writing a novel herself, she'd finished it in two months and, thanks to her sister's superior agenting skills, sold it in two days!

Crazy Quilt was a cozy mystery set in Maine, where Emma had lived for years. The amateur sleuth was a quilting instructor and owner of a craft supply store. Emma's publisher envisioned it as the first of a series and had signed her for two more books. Her lifelong love of mystery novels and innate storytelling ability had served her well.

Logan turned to Gage. "Zara tells me *Incision*'s going to be made into a movie. It's a hell of a book—it'll be dynamite on the big screen."

"Thanks, but your missus deserves the credit for the movie deal, and for that new multibook contract she just negotiated for me." He winked at his new sister-in-law. "Lady, those fellas in New York and Hollywood must run for cover when they see you comin'."

Zara and Logan exchanged a private grin. She said, "Like cockroaches."

Logan slipped his arm around her. "I thought it was cheap panty hose."

Candy snorted. "What would Zara know about panty hose?"

Billy said, "If we can move the subject away from my daughter's unmentionables, I have an announcement to make. My wife—" he put his arm around

Candy's shoulders and pulled her close "—has been asked to star in three exercise videos, aimed at the mature set. Jane Fonda, watch out!"

Candy accepted her family's heartfelt congratulations. She basked in her husband's pride. He'd harassed and cajoled her every step of the way. If not for him, she wouldn't have found the gumption to fight for this long-held dream.

The photographer returned with Logan's and Gage's parents. The Fosters were warm and gregarious as always, but Madeline and Douglas Byrne looked ill at ease as they approached the group, as if intruding on a stranger's celebration. Candy's heart went out to them. As a parent, she empathized with what they'd gone through, both before and after Mac's death. She took the fact that they'd agreed to attend Logan's wedding as a positive omen.

Douglas offered his hand, and Logan shook it. "I'm happy for you, son. She's a wonderful girl." The emotion that flowed between them as they stared into each other's eyes brought a lump to Candy's throat.

Madeline Byrne tentatively touched her son's fingers. He covered her hand with both of his, hesitated a moment and pulled her into his arms. He whispered hoarsely, "I love you, Mom," and tightened his hold.

Candy caught Zara's eye, saw the sheen of tears and answered her wobbly smile with one of her own. It was a first step. It wouldn't be easy. These three had a painful past to overcome and a long journey ahead of them. But she sensed an underlying devotion that would see them through.

The photographer had positioned his tripod and

was busy posing the group. "Gentlemen in back, ladies in front. Arms at your sides. Turn a little that way. Move in, please. Closer. Closer."

Emma gave a little gasp and smirked over her shoulder at her new husband.

Gage's grin was unrepentant. "The man said to get closer, darlin'."

"He didn't mean your *hands!*"

Billy, too, was surreptitiously fondling his wife's bottom, but did *she* complain?

The band struck up the lively "Dippermouth Blues" as the photographer scanned his subjects one last time and peered through the viewfinder. "Okay, now, everyone smile."

That part was easy, Candy thought. They all had something to smile about.

HE SAID

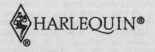

SHE SAID

Explore the mystery of male/female communication in this extraordinary new book from two of your favorite Harlequin authors.

Jasmine Cresswell and Margaret St. George bring you the exciting story of two romantic adversaries—each from their own point of view!

DEV'S STORY. CATHY'S STORY.
As he sees it. As she sees it.
Both sides of the story!

The heat is definitely on, and these two can't stay out of the kitchen!

Don't miss **HE SAID, SHE SAID.**
Available in July wherever Harlequin books are sold.

HARLEQUIN®

MILLION DOLLAR SWEEPSTAKES
OFFICIAL RULES
NO PURCHASE NECESSARY TO ENTER

1. To enter, follow the directions published. Method of entry may vary. For eligibility, entries must be received no later than March 31, 1998. No liability is assumed for printing errors, lost, late, non-delivered or misdirected entries.

   To determine winners, the sweepstakes numbers assigned to submitted entries will be compared against a list of randomly, preselected prize winning numbers. In the event all prizes are not claimed via the return of prize winning numbers, random drawings will be held from among all other entries received to award unclaimed prizes.

2. Prize winners will be determined no later than June 30, 1998. Selection of winning numbers and random drawings are under the supervision of D. L. Blair, Inc., an independent judging organization whose decisions are final. Limit: one prize to a family or organization. No substitution will be made for any prize, except as offered. Taxes and duties on all prizes are the sole responsibility of winners. Winners will be notified by mail. Odds of winning are determined by the number of eligible entries distributed and received.

3. Sweepstakes open to residents of the U.S. (except Puerto Rico), Canada and Europe who are 18 years of age or older, except employees and immediate family members of Torstar Corp., D. L. Blair, Inc., their affiliates, subsidiaries, and all other agencies, entities, and persons connected with the use, marketing or conduct of this sweepstakes. All applicable laws and regulations apply. Sweepstakes offer void wherever prohibited by law. Any litigation within the province of Quebec respecting the conduct and awarding of a prize in this sweepstakes must be submitted to the Régie des alcools, des courses et des jeux. In order to win a prize, residents of Canada will be required to correctly answer a time-limited arithmetical skill-testing question to be administered by mail.

4. Winners of major prizes (Grand through Fourth) will be obligated to sign and return an Affidavit of Eligibility and Release of Liability within 30 days of notification. In the event of non-compliance within this time period or if a prize is returned as undeliverable, D. L. Blair, Inc. may at its sole discretion, award that prize to an alternate winner. By acceptance of their prize, winners consent to use of their names, photographs or other likeness for purposes of advertising, trade and promotion on behalf of Torstar Corp., its affiliates and subsidiaries, without further compensation unless prohibited by law. Torstar Corp. and D. L. Blair, Inc., their affiliates and subsidiaries are not responsible for errors in printing of sweepstakes and prize winning numbers. In the event a duplication of a prize winning number occurs, a random drawing will be held from among all entries received with that prize winning number to award that prize.

5. This sweepstakes is presented by Torstar Corp., its subsidiaries and affiliates in conjunction with book, merchandise and/or product offerings. The number of prizes to be awarded and their value are as follows: Grand Prize — $1,000,000 (payable at $33,333.33 a year for 30 years); First Prize — $50,000; Second Prize — $10,000; Third Prize — $5,000; 3 Fourth Prizes — $1,000 each; 10 Fifth Prizes — $250 each; 1,000 Sixth Prizes — $10 each. Values of all prizes are in U.S. currency. Prizes in each level will be presented in different creative executions, including various currencies, vehicles, merchandise and travel. Any presentation of a prize level in a currency other than U.S. currency represents an approximate equivalent to the U.S. currency prize for that level, at that time. Prize winners will have the opportunity of selecting any prize offered for that level; however, the actual non U.S. currency equivalent prize if offered and selected, shall be awarded at the exchange rate existing at 3:00 P.M. New York time on March 31, 1998. A travel prize option, if offered and selected by winner, must be completed within 12 months of selection and is subject to: traveling companion(s) completing and returning of a Release of Liability prior to travel; and hotel and flight accommodations availability. For a current list of all prize options offered within prize levels, send a self-addressed, stamped envelope (WA residents need not affix postage) to: MILLION DOLLAR SWEEPSTAKES Prize Options, P.O. Box 4456, Blair, NE 68009-4456, USA.

6. For a list of prize winners (available after July 31, 1998) send a separate, stamped, self-addressed envelope to: MILLION DOLLAR SWEEPSTAKES Winners, P.O. Box 4459, Blair, NE 68009-4459, USA.

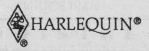

Imagine that you've traveled far away, to a place of heady danger and luxurious romance nestled high in the Colorado Rocky Mountains. The bellhop has left your bags, and you're about to unpack in a room you'll share with a sexy man....

Welcome to the

Honeymoon Hideaway

This summer, reader favorite Sheryl Lynn brings you this exciting duet in June and July. Don't miss her upcoming romantic mysteries:

#424 THE CASE OF THE VANISHED GROOM
#425 THE CASE OF THE BAD LUCK FIANCÉ

Harlequin Intrigue invites you to make your vacation escape to the HONEYMOON HIDEAWAY!

 HARLEQUIN®

I N T R I G U E ®

HMH

COMING NEXT MONTH

#421 SWORN TO SILENCE by Vickie York
Lawman

When intelligence officer Erin Meyer wrongfully intercepted a message pertaining to an assassination, she had no choice but to save the man's life. But now Dan Donovan was stealing her heart...and the life she saved might be her own!

#422 ALIAS: DADDY by Adrianne Lee
Hidden Identity

While attempting to meet a killer who chose victims through the personals, cop Kerrie Muldoon got a "blind date" with old flame Nick Diamond. Years ago Nick harbored secrets that made him look guilty; now Kerrie is keeping secrets, too—their daughters.

#423 ONE TOUGH TEXAN by M.J. Rodgers

Matt Bonner was a "finder of lost loves," but the man Jamie Lee was looking for—the man who'd given her her first kiss—didn't exist. Why then was his trail strewn with danger, destruction and undeniable desire? Unless there was more to that kiss than Jamie Lee was willing to tell....

#424 THE CASE OF THE VANISHED GROOM by Sheryl Lynn
Honeymoon Hideaway

The morning after her wedding Dawn Lovell awakened to find the man next to her in bed was her husband's best man. Had her husband robbed her and vanished—or been the victim of foul play? Ross Duke seemed set on finding Dawn's spouse guilty—but was it only because *he* wanted to marry Dawn?

AVAILABLE THIS MONTH:

Free Gift Offer

With a Free Gift proof-of-purchase
from any Harlequin® book, you can receive
a beautiful cubic zirconia pendant.

This stunning marquise-shaped stone is a genuine cubic
zirconia—accented by an 18" gold tone necklace.
(Approximate retail value $19.95)

Send for yours today...
compliments of ◆HARLEQUIN®

To receive your free gift, a cubic zirconia pendant, send us one original proof-of-
purchase, photocopies not accepted, from the back of any Harlequin Romance®,
Harlequin Presents®, Harlequin Temptation®, Harlequin Superromance®, Harlequin
Intrigue®, Harlequin American Romance®, or Harlequin Historicals® title available at
your favorite retail outlet, together with the Free Gift Certificate, plus a check or money
order for $1.65 U.S./$2.15 CAN. (do not send cash) to cover postage and handling,
payable to Harlequin Free Gift Offer. We will send you the specified gift. Allow 6 to 8
weeks for delivery. Offer good until December 31, 1997, or while quantities last. Offer
valid in the U.S. and Canada only.

Free Gift Certificate

Name: _____

Address: _____

City: _____ State/Province: _____ Zip/Postal Code: _____

Mail this certificate, one proof-of-purchase and a check or money order for postage
and handling to: HARLEQUIN FREE GIFT OFFER 1997. In the U.S.: 3010 Walden
Avenue, P.O. Box 9071, Buffalo NY 14269-9057. In Canada: P.O. Box 604, Fort Erie,
Ontario L2Z 5X3.

FREE GIFT OFFER   084-KEZ

ONE PROOF-OF-PURCHASE
To collect your fabulous FREE GIFT, a cubic zirconia pendant, you must include this
original proof-of-purchase for each gift with the properly completed Free Gift Certificate.

084-KEZR